How To
Blackmail a
Highlander

The MacGregor Lairds

How To
Blackmail a

The MacGregor Lairds

Michelle
McLean

Entangled Publishing, LLC
2614 South Timberline Road
Suite 105, PMB 159
Fort Collins, CO 80525
rights@entangledpublishing.com

Scandalous is an imprint of Entangled Publishing, LLC.

Edited by Erin Molta
Cover design by EDH Graphics
Cover photography from 123.rf and Depositphotos

Manufactured in the United States of America

First Edition January 2019

SCANDALOUS

To the ginger I love

Chapter One

Lady Alice Chivers twirled across the dance floor, rather bemused at how she could be so ecstatically happy and so full of despair at the same time. She was in her element. Surrounded by lovely men, clad in a stunning new gown that showed off all her best assets, with a gaggle of her best friends giggling in the background as she flirted with her many suitors. The music swelled louder with each swish of her skirts, and for a moment she wished she hadn't had her maid lace her up quite so tight. Drawing a breath grew more and more difficult with each turn.

But she wanted to look her best tonight. For her last hurrah. Reginald Nash, the eighth Earl of Woolsmere, had proposed, and her excited parents had immediately accepted. The engagement would be announced soon. But tonight...tonight was hers. She was still young, and officially unattached, and she was going to enjoy herself.

She smiled at the man who held her. James—or perhaps it was John...or Jasper—gazed down at her and squeezed her hand tighter. They spun, and Alice caught her mother's disapproving gaze. She fought down the bubble of unease that threatened to erupt. It was a simple dance. Harmless. Perfectly acceptable. And she was enjoying every second of it.

After all, it would probably be the last time she would experience a handsome young man's arms about her. The sensation of his breath on her skin as he leaned down to talk to her. She wished she could rip the gloves from their fingers so just once she might feel his skin against her own. Perhaps they could steal into an alcove and share a forbidden kiss.

She'd like to know the touch of a virile young gentleman. Once in her life. Before she was shackled to the decrepit, flatulent, and likely murderous lord her parents had chosen for her to wed.

The words she'd shared with her best friend, Lady Elizabet Dawsey, when she'd been in the same situation, came back to haunt her. She'd told Elizabet that she'd be lucky to marry an old man. After all, the older he was, the more likely it was that he'd leave her an independent widow all the sooner. A little more difficult to be excited about that prospect, however, when she was the one facing marriage to a man old enough to be her grandfather. One who'd already buried three wives much younger than he. Not only was the possibility of a happy marriage nonexistent, the likelihood she'd outlive her husband was questionable. At least if the gossips could be believed. And no matter what her mother said, the gossips were rarely wrong.

Another spin brought her mother into focus again, but Alice paid her no mind. She pressed herself a little closer to her partner, surprised at her own boldness, and focused solely on the deep, chocolate brown eyes that gazed into hers.

"You have a most curious expression on that pretty face of yours, my lady," he said. "Might I inquire as to its meaning?"

Alice smiled at him. "I was wishing that this dance might

go on forever."

His hand pressed her closer. "I wish the same thing."

But already the music was drawing to a close. A final twirl, a promenade, and they bowed, slightly breathless and all smiles.

"Perhaps I could call on you tomorrow?" he asked.

She sighed. "That would be lovely, but I'm afraid it won't be possible. My mother has arranged a prior engagement."

The music came to an end, and Alice reluctantly released him. Their hands lingered together for the briefest moment, unnoticed by anyone. Or so Alice thought. In her absorption, she hadn't noticed that they'd stopped right in front of her mother. By the expression on her face, Alice's mother hadn't missed anything that had passed between her daughter and her dance partner.

Alice clasped her hands together and kept her gaze on the floor while her mother addressed them.

"Mr. Sinclair. How good to see you. I hadn't realized you were acquainted with my daughter."

"Good evening, Lady Morely," he said, giving her a gallant bow. "I hadn't been before this evening. Something I'm glad was remedied. She is delightful."

He smiled at her, and Alice tried to return the expression, though the sour turn of her mother's lips made that difficult.

"Yes," her mother agreed. "She's had quite the Season. No less than three proposals."

Mr. Sinclair's—Jeremy? Jason?—smile faded slightly. "I am not surprised at all. I'm sure any gentleman would be proud to have Lady Alice on his arm."

"Indeed." Her mother nodded and leaned in as if she were about to impart some great secret. "In fact, we will be making an announcement very soon. We're thrilled, of course."

He shot a surprised look at Alice, who tried not to flinch

against the sudden spike of guilt, and then he gave her mother a tight smile. "I can well imagine. My lady…" He turned and gave Alice a rigid bow with another toward her mother. "It's been a pleasure."

Alice watched him until he was out of sight. Then she risked a glance at her mother. And wished she hadn't.

"I'll speak to you later," Lady Morely said with a snap of her fan. "But for now, someone else would like a moment of your attention."

She nodded toward where Woolsmere stood with a few of his decrepit cronies, and Alice's stomach sank as his thin lips stretched over his yellowed teeth. Her mother linked her arm through Alice's and leaned in to whisper. But much to Alice's surprise, instead of the admonishment for her behavior that Alice expected, her mother's voice was soft and almost sympathetic.

"He's wealthy, well connected, and will elevate you further than we ever dreamed," her mother whispered to her behind her fan. "Smile and bear it, my child. Like we all must do."

Before Alice could say anything else, they'd reached Woolsmere, and her mother deposited her and then gracefully drifted toward her guests.

"My lord," Alice said, gritting her teeth and dropping into a quick bob. "I trust you are enjoying your evening."

"Indeed," Woolsmere said, taking her elbow in a painful grip and leading her out of earshot of the other guests. "Though I'm not enjoying myself nearly as much as you seem to be, my dear."

Alice's gaze shot to his, and he leered down at her. "No matter," he muttered, his foul breath wafting over her face. He leaned in even closer, and she steeled herself to keep from cringing away. "There's no harm in enjoying yourself a bit, I suppose. As long as you restrict it to a public dance or two." His eyes roved over her body. "After all, soon enough I'll be the one enjoying the pleasures of your flesh. I can be generous for one last night. Once this ripe body of yours is swelling with my child you won't have time for such frivolous concerns. Best to get them out of your system now. Once we are wed, you'll become accustomed to a quieter life in the country."

Alice drew in a strangled breath through her pinched nostrils but couldn't stop a retort from leaving her lips. "And what if I prove to be as barren as your other wives?" she asked, refusing to flinch when he glared at her.

He tightened his grip on her arm until she sucked in a pained breath. Then he shrugged. "You aren't the only field where I can plow my seed. Merely the cheapest bought." He nodded with a falsely magnanimous smile at where her mother stood watching them.

Alice jerked her arm out of his grasp but before she could give in to her emotions and punch the old goat in the throat as he so richly deserved, her sister Mary flounced to her side, her ringlets bobbing over her ears.

"Alice, there you are! My lord, would you mind terribly if I stole my sister away?"

"Of course not, my dear," Woolsmere said, aiming that sickly false grin at her. "I'll have her all to myself soon enough."

Mary giggled, though Alice could tell it was forced, and quickly led her away from her soon-to-be-betrothed.

Their mother frowned at them and subtly jerked her head back in Woolsmere's direction. But there was no way Alice was subjecting herself to him again, now that she'd escaped. She took Mary's hand, thrust her chin in the air, and marched off in the opposite direction of Woolsmere and her mother.

"Ah, you'll pay for that," Mary said once they'd found a quiet corner.

Alice sighed. "I'm already paying for it. They can't punish me more than they already have."

"Marriage to one of the richest men at court is hardly a punishment."

"I heartily disagree. And so do you, or you wouldn't have rescued me."

Mary snorted. "I rather think I was rescuing Woolsmere, going by the look on your face when I intervened."

Alice laughed and gave her sister a quick hug. "Yes, well, perhaps you rescued us both."

"I would think you'd be happy. He's wealthy and well-connected, and marrying him will make you a countess. Isn't that what you always wanted?"

Alice frowned. "Once, perhaps. But I suppose I never considered the price I'd have to pay to get it. My dreams never included being a broodmare to a controlling lecher who makes my skin crawl."

Mary's exasperated sigh was not without sympathy. "Men marry to get heirs. You can't truly be surprised that you'd be expected to provide one."

"Of course not. But..." Alice's eyes darted around the room to make sure no one stood too close, and she leaned toward her sister. "None of his previous wives were able to give him a child. Perhaps the problem does not lie with the women he married. And then they each died within a few years of marrying him. Seems a convenient way to rid himself of a wife, for perhaps his failing."

Her sister frowned at that and whispered, "You think he murdered his wives for failing to provide him with an heir?"

"All I know is that Woolsmere buried his last three wives in the country almost the moment he married them. Both figuratively and literally. None of them were seen at court again once they were wed."

"Perhaps he prefers the quiet country life."

Alice shook her head. "He may say that. But Rose told me one of the stable boys at Woolsmere's estate heard from one of the upstairs maids that he made his wives follow a strict set of rules and even locked them in their chambers at night to ensure they couldn't run away. They say there were horrible rows over the lack of an heir. And each of his wives died mysteriously."

Her sister scoffed. "Those are naught but mean-spirited tales. If there was any truth to any of it, surely something would have been done."

"They are not tales. They are eyewitness accounts."

Mary's lips pursed at that, but she didn't argue. "You shouldn't be gossiping with your maid and the other servants."

"Why not? They see and know everything."

"You truly believe he murdered his wives?"

"I'm saying it seems suspicious, is all. For three women to all die so young, not in childbirth… And just now, Woolsmere implied I'd be easily replaced."

She was silent for a moment, but then Mary shook her head. "Mother and Father would never marry you off to a man they suspected might harm you. They might be ambitious, but they do care for us. The tales about Woolsmere's previous wives are merely that. Tales."

"Well, I'd rather not be proven right and be the fourth wife he buries. Difficult to say *I told you* so from my grave."

Mary narrowed her eyes. "Well, murderous deviant or not, even if you weren't practically engaged, flirting with every man in attendance probably isn't the wisest course of action."

Alice shrugged. "I've done nothing wrong. I merely danced with him. And a few others."

"A few?" her sister said, laughing.

Alice couldn't help smiling. "There is certainly no law against that. Besides, she is the one who insisted we come tonight."

"True. Though I don't think she'll see it that way. I doubt she expected you to chase after every unmarried man in the room."

Alice feigned bravado. "I have precious few days of freedom left. I shall do with them as I please."

"It might not be as bad as all that. There's no need to be quite so dramatic."

Alice raised a brow. "Again, I disagree. There is every need."

"If any of the tales about how Woolsmere treated his wives were true, surely someone would have tried to help."

"Who could do anything? There's no proof he murdered any of them, damning circumstantial evidence notwithstanding, and he's well within his husbandly rights to treat his wives as horribly as he pleases."

"Well, that doesn't mean he'll be horrible to you."

"*Um hmm*," Alice murmured, one eyebrow cocked.

Mary gave her a quick hug. "Either way, ruining your reputation now won't help matters at all. So, behave."

She gave her a little wave and flounced off in search of more entertaining company.

Alice tried to keep the grimace from her face as she scanned the crowd. She longed for her best friend with an aching sadness. She and Elizabet had been as close as she and Mary, closer even, and while it warmed Alice's heart to know that Elizabet was happy, she felt the loss of her keenly.

Then again, she didn't know for certain that Elizabet was happy. She was with her love, so Alice assumed…hoped. But she had been gone nearly a year with no word. The more time that passed, the more fear crept in—perhaps all had *not* gone well with her friend's escape. She'd run off with John MacGregor, otherwise known as the notorious Highland Highwayman, when he'd been exiled from England, so Alice certainly had cause for concern. But John loved Elizabet more than anything in the world, and Elizabet felt the same about him. He'd already nearly perished once to keep Elizabet safe. Alice prayed they were healthy and happy together... somewhere.

She took a breath of the suddenly stifling air in the ballroom and fanned herself with a touch more vigor. A slight breeze from the open French doors beckoned her. But she got no farther than the monstrous potted plants that guarded the doorways before someone's arm shot out and hauled her into the secluded recess behind the plant, a hand firmly clamped over her mouth.

Chapter Two

Alice struggled, driving an elbow into the rock-solid chest she was held against. It drew a muffled *oof* from her large captor but didn't loosen his grip. Her small heel grinding into his boot resulted in a satisfying grunt of pain, but again, no freedom.

"Be still, ye wee wildcat," his deep voice rumbled in her ear. "I've a message for ye from the Lady Elizabet."

At that, Alice struggled again, not to get away, but in overwhelming excitement.

The arm around her waist tightened. "Be still," he said again. "I'll release ye if ye promise not to make a sound, aye?"

She nodded as hard as she could with his hand engulfing most of her face.

His hands slid slowly away, and she turned in his arms before he'd fully released her.

"Do ye remember me?"

"I don't…" She squinted at him, and then her heart jumped in her chest. "Yes! You're John's kinsman? I saw you when you came to Bess's house, when you brought her word of him."

"Aye," he said with a pleased smile. "Philip MacGregor, my lady."

"You have a message from Bess? Truly?"

He nodded and pulled the sealed letter from his coat pocket. She seized it and held it to her chest for a moment before looking back up at him with a grin so wide it hurt her cheeks.

"Thank you," she said. She jumped at him, throwing her arms about his neck so she could press a hard, fast kiss to his mouth.

He pulled away but kept his arms about her, glancing at her with something akin to horrified shock. Though a small smile tugged at his lips.

"Ye're welcome, my lady."

Her happiness was somewhat eclipsed by the feel of his strong arms about her, and she took him in fully. His coat, vest, and breeches were tasteful enough, if a bit out of fashion and threadbare. And with that accent, she'd half expected to see a kilt swirling about his legs rather than the tightly fitting breeches. Though a kilt would have stood out among her parents' guests and judging from the way he hid behind the potted plants on the terrace, being noticed wasn't what he was after.

Probably a wise choice, because there would be no escaping notice, no matter what he wore. His broad arms and chest suggested a man who was more used to physical labor than gracing soirees and tea parties, but his face... The strong, chiseled features framed by dark, nearly black hair, were handsome on their own merit. Disturbingly so. But his startlingly blue eyes sent a fine tremor through her that had nothing to do with fear. She could gaze at his face forever.

Her hands tightened slightly on his arms, and she tried to mask the trouble she seemed to have breathing. She'd always believed in following her impulses, savoring every moment life offered. Doing so seemed more important now than ever with her uncertain future looming before her. Still, she couldn't help the voice in her head that urged caution. The man who still held her, whose presence sent her heart racing, might be a complete scoundrel. A criminal. He'd ridden at John's side, after all. His righthand man and most trusted cohort. A highwayman, though he'd never been convicted. While John was an honorable man, Philip might be a sadistic, cruel bastard of the worst kind. Though she highly doubted that was true.

And inner voice or not, she had trouble caring. She'd never been so utterly captivated by a man before. The urge to wrap herself about him was astonishingly strong, even for her impulsive nature. Were it not for the fact that they stood on her parents' terrace—and the fact that the man in question might protest—she would throw her arms about his neck and express more than her gratefulness at his delivery of Elizabet's letter.

Elizabet!

She jerked away from him, glancing down at the letter.

"Dinna let anyone see that," he warned. "There are still those who wish them harm."

"Of course," she said, trying to keep her tone civil. What did he take her for? "I'd never put Elizabet in harm's way." She carefully tucked the letter down the front of her gown. "There. All safe and snug."

Philip glanced at her chest and then met her gaze. The heat in his eyes made her swallow hard against her suddenly dry mouth.

She cleared her throat. "May I send a response?"

He nodded, his gaze boring into hers. "I'll be waiting in yer stables tomorrow at sunrise. Most of the house will likely still be abed then. I'll no' wait long, so dinna tarry."

"I'll be there." She hesitated for a moment, and then gave in to temptation. She rose on her toes and pressed another quick kiss to his lips. "Thank you, Philip. Truly."

Though his eyes widened slightly in surprise, he took her hand and pressed a lingering kiss to it. "'Tis my pleasure, my lady." He took a few steps back, melting into the shadows. "Until tomorrow."

Alice waited until she knew he was gone, one hand hovering at her lips, which still tingled from his touch. The other pressed to her bodice and the precious letter inside. Waiting until she could excuse herself to read it would be torture.

Unfortunately, she had to wait much longer than she'd anticipated.

Mary had been right. Mother's fury surpassed anything Alice had suffered before. The party guests had gone, and the clock had long since struck midnight. Alice shifted, longing to escape the confines of her boned bodice and heeled slippers. She had already endured a thirty-minute harangue for her behavior. She wasn't sure how much more she could take.

"It's a good thing Lord Woolsmere is a forgiving man," her mother said for the tenth time. "What he thought of his fiancée throwing herself at every man on the dance floor, I have no idea. And then coming in from the terrace, flushed and disheveled. One can only begin to guess at what you were doing out there."

"Mother, I told you, I needed a bit of air. And I wasn't disheveled. A branch from the tree by the door caught in my hair. That is all. And I danced only once with each man who asked! That is perfectly acceptable."

"Oh yes. You danced. With hardly a breath of space between you while you whispered nonsense to each and every one!"

"That's not true!"

"It is true! I've a good mind to send formal complaints to quite a few of those so-called gentlemen!"

"Mother, you can't do that! I know you are cross with me, but you can't taint anyone's reputation for some imagined infraction."

Lady Morely paused for a moment, and the fight seemed to drain out of her. "No. I wouldn't. Though I don't believe for a moment that your 'infraction,' as you put it, was imagined. And I'll refrain only because it would be your reputation that would end up the worse for it, and it's already damaged enough after tonight's debacle." She walked over and slumped onto the sofa, leaning back against the cushions with a tired sigh.

"Come sit by me," she said, patting the cushion next to her.

Alice hesitated, not sure if she trusted this calmer version of her mother. She went to the sofa and perched on the edge. Lady Morely sat up and took her hands.

"Alice, my dear child. Whatever you may think of me, I have your best interest at heart. I know Woolsmere is old and not particularly attractive. But his fortune and good name will enable you to live in luxury all your life. There is little enough I can do for you in this world. Ensuring you marry well is the best way I can secure your future. It may not seem so now, but you are a very lucky girl. Don't throw your life away over some fantasized notion of love. It doesn't exist. Comfort and security are far more important."

Alice weighed her words carefully. She knew her mother had her best interests at heart, and most would consider that her parents had done very well for her. But she couldn't shake the niggling fears at the back of her mind. There had been too much gossip, too many unanswered questions. And Woolsmere himself seemed to confirm all her fears. She could be honest enough to admit that if it weren't her own life hanging in the balance, she might even be watching this new betrothal unfold with interest. But if the gossips weren't wrong, she wouldn't be able to shake her head sadly and murmur about the strangeness of yet another Woolsmere bride dying.

Her mother waited, her eyes searching Alice's face. Alice cast her gaze downward, not trusting her expression. "I know you've made the best match for me that you could. And I'm grateful. Truly. But…the stories…"

Lady Morely held up a hand. "I'll not entertain any such nonsense. You've allowed salacious gossip to color your opinions. Yes, it's true that the earl has been married before."

"Three times," Alice started, but her mother held up her hand again.

"Yes, and isn't it horrible for him that's he's had to bury three wives? The scandalmongers want to make much more of it than is there. Accidents and illnesses are commonplace. There is nothing suspicious about any of it. You can't possibly believe that I'd willingly send you into danger, do you?"

Alice frowned at that. It was the one aspect of it all that she struggled with the most. She truly didn't believe her parents would knowingly put her in harm's way. But that didn't mean her parents weren't wrong, nor did it alleviate her fears about Woolsmere.

Her mother waited for an answer, her face pained. Alice sighed. "Of course not, Mother. But—"

"That's my good girl," Lady Morely said, deftly putting an end to whatever else Alice had been meaning to say. She pulled her close to bestow a rare kiss on her brow. "Now, hurry up to bed."

Alice bit her lip to keep from snapping back in frustration. She finally managed to say, "Yes, Mother," and flounced off to her room, the sound of her mother's long-suffering sigh ringing in her head.

Alice's feet dragged up the stairs, every step taking her closer to the life she dreaded.

She missed Elizabet. She would understand.

But she wasn't here anymore. She'd had the courage to run away with her love. To start a new life far from those who would dictate how she'd live. She'd promised to write, but Alice hadn't heard a word from her since the night she'd jumped on a ship with her exiled highwayman and disappeared from England forever. If Alice knew where she was, perhaps she could run away as well. Surely Elizabet would offer her shelter.

She reached her room and immediately kicked off her slippers. Her maid, Rose, rushed over to help her remove the heavy ball gown. Elizabet's letter fell to the ground and Rose quickly retrieved it.

"My lady," she said, handing it to her.

"Thank you." She took it and dismissed Rose for the night. Then she jumped into her warm bed and settled back against the pillows so she could devour every word.

Once she'd read it, she read it again. And again. She could hear her friend's voice in her head as she read the words, and it brought a smile to her face. Elizabet was safe. And happy. So very happy.

Alice finally lay back against her pillows with a sigh. She wished Elizabet was here. Or, more accurately, she wished she were with Elizabet. As that didn't seem to be possible, she was at least grateful Philip had taken the risk to bring her word. She needed to write a response before he arrived at dawn the next morning.

Philip.

Friend and cousin to Elizabet's love John MacGregor. She would be safe with such a man as Philip by her side. Elizabet had told her tales of John's men and her adventures with them when she'd spent time under John's care. Philip was surely an honorable man. A highwayman once, yes. But he and the Highland Highwayman's gang had never harmed anyone. On the whole, they had divested a few querulous noblemen of their ill-gotten gains and had returned the money or jewels to their rightful owners. Or those who desperately needed the money gained from them.

No, Philip was strong, brave, and dependable. A man she could rely on, she was sure of it. One she'd never have to fear. One who made her blood run hot with spine-tingling possibilities, rather than making it run cold with revulsion.

As much as she hated it, she needed a man to get by in the world in which she lived. But she'd be damned if she would let someone else choose that man for her. Her fate would be in her own hands.

A daring plan began to form in Alice's mind. She wouldn't sleep a wink waiting for the dawn and Philip's return.

Chapter Three

Philip MacGregor clasped his hands behind him and stared at the clearly mad young woman in front of him, unable to muster more of a response than a slow blink.

"Well," Lady Alice said. "What is your answer?"

He gave a little shake of his head. "I'm sorry. I didna realize that ridiculous notion ye uttered was a serious question that required a response."

She drew herself up, jutting that haughty chin in the air. "And why, may I ask, is my request ridiculous?"

"Ye canna be serious."

"I'm deadly serious."

His response to that was a derisive snort.

"So, you're refusing to help me?"

"Of course I'm refusing, ye daft madwoman. If ye want to run away from yer home and kin, ye'll have to do it on yer own. Helping ye would make me little better than a kidnapper, and I've enough trouble with the law as it is."

"You helped Lady Elizabet. You did more than help her. You came to fetch her. Put the idea in her head. All but led her to the ship and tossed her aboard," she said, crossing her arms across her tantalizingly rosy bosom. Her pale skin flushed the more agitated she became. And it wasn't solely her cheeks that were affected. Every ounce of skin that showed, and there was a considerable amount in her fashionable, low-cut gown, was tinged a becoming pink that complemented the auburn hue of her ringleted hair.

Philip snapped himself out of it. He'd always found the Lady Alice visually appealing, since he'd first seen her when he'd helped John and the Lady Elizabet. But the woman was too spoiled and headstrong for his tastes. Not that he liked his women docile. Quite the opposite. But the lady before him was pampered and too used to getting her own way. Which meant getting her to accept his refusal would be damn near impossible.

"The Lady Elizabet's situation was far different than this," he said, exerting considerable effort to keep his emotions under control and not shout. He really wanted to shake some sense into the lass.

"Elizabet was being forced to wed someone she didn't love, and you helped her escape it."

"I helped her escape the murderous criminal her father was going to shackle her to. That's a far sight different than yer situation, and ye ken it well. She wasna planning on running off into the wild with no one to keep her safe because she didna particularly like the gentleman her parents had chosen. The man her father had chosen would have gladly killed her on their wedding night. Can ye say the same?"

Alice stuck her chin in the air. "Actually—"

He gave a sharp nod of his head, not needing to hear the rest. "Ye may not like yer intended, but he's no danger to ye, and a fair sight better than many men would be, I'd wager."

"But that's not tr—"

"Ye'll probably be coddled and pampered all yer days.

The best thing for ye is to stay put. Living rough is no life for a lady."

"But Elizabet—"

"Had my laird to protect her and no other choice, if she wanted to live."

"Neither do I, if I want a shred of happiness in my life. The tales of how Woolsmere treated his previous wives would be reason enough for me to want to escape. But their mysterious fates…"

"Are naught but gossip and hearsay."

"You've never spoken to the man! He all but admitted it to me and implied it would be my fate as well, should I fail him. And I'd rather not marry him and find out that the tales *were* true. I'd be too dead to enjoy proving you wrong!"

That stopped him for a moment. She had a point. He certainly wouldn't want to marry a woman who'd buried multiple husbands within a few years of marriage. He also had no doubt a man with Woolsmere's money and connections could make even the worst crimes evaporate. But surely the lady's parents wouldn't have arranged the marriage if they'd feared for their daughter. It still wasn't any of his concern. He'd simply have to ignore the pit of unease growing in his stomach and go on about his life. Before the distracting lady who stood before him used up what little luck he had left and got him locked up for good. Or worse.

"You may not believe me, but I don't have any more choice than Elizabet did if I want to live. And I'd have you to protect me."

Philip scowled. "No. Ye don't."

She opened her mouth to argue some more, but he'd heard enough. He held up his hand and clapped his cap back on his head. "Since ye have no direct message for my lady, other than yer desire to join her in exile, I'll be takin' my leave."

He gave her a stiff bow and turned to march out. "Good day," he said, departing before she could say another word.

His kinsman Will waited outside the stables with his horse. He handed Philip the reins and mounted his own horse, eyebrow raised in question. Philip scowled again.

"Dinna ask," Philip said.

Will raised the other eyebrow. Philip let out a huge, exasperated breath. "These English women are all mad as barn cats. First, the Lady Sorcha and what she put Malcolm through when they wed. Then Lady Elizabet with John, and now Lady Alice and her daft ideas. Her High and Mightiness demanding that I help her run away. From what? A pampered life in London's finest palaces? So she can go live like a crofter in some Scottish backwoods? She wouldna last the trip, let alone once she got there. All because they listen to idle gossip and get romantic foolishness in their heads and canna think of anything else. As if marrying a man who is willing to support them in luxury for the rest of their days is the most terrible thing to happen to a lass. The notion! There's more to marriage than love, and I reckon it's time she learned that."

"Aye," Will said, his tone both agreeing and confused. "Though, doesna the Lion and his lady love each other now? And my laird John and the Lady Elizabet?"

Philip waved that off. "My reasoning stands. Malcolm may have the fortune of having found happiness with his wife, but it didna start that way. They had to wed at the command of their king, and so they did because that is what reasonable folk do."

"So ye'd marry a lass who'd been chosen for ye? Without argument or complaint?"

Philip grimaced. "That's a different matter. I've never been one for marriage, and I doubt any lassie would have me. But aye, if my laird commanded it of me, I'd do my duty and keep my mouth shut about it. Not like this flighty English lass who's taking it into her head to challenge the very men who are responsible for her comfort and well-being."

Will nodded in agreement. "I prefer a quiet, obedient lass. The Lion and Laird John may be happy with their spirited wives, but I wouldna want such a woman."

"Ha!" Philip said, clapping Will on the back. "'Tis only because Lady Elizabet bested ye when ye first rode with us and were supposed to be guarding our backs. Slipping past ye when ye were takin' a piss, and then busting that pretty nose on yer face when ye tried to stop her."

Will glared at him, which made Philip laugh harder. Will was a good lad but still had much growing to do. Including taking responsibility for his mistakes. Between Lady Sorcha turning Castle Glenlyon upside down when she'd first arrived and Lady Elizabet physically besting him and making a fool of him in the process, Will had decided that the only good woman was a docile lass who wouldna give him a lick of trouble.

He might have to deal with less aggravation with a woman like that. But he'd also miss out on the passion that drove that kind of behavior.

Then again—with the scene between him and Lady Alice fresh in his mind—a quiet, docile woman might not be such a bad thing. At least he'd turned her down. He'd tell Lady Elizabet that her friend missed her but would soon be wed to a worthy—or esteemed and wealthy, at the very least—gentleman and leave it at that. He'd let the lady's parents ensure her safety and happiness, as was their place, and wash his hands of the whole business.

• • •

Alice paced her room, swishing aside the curtains to peek outside every time she passed them. Finally, she caught sight of her maid hurrying through the gate of the townhouse. She continued her pacing until the maid knocked rapidly on the door before opening it.

"Did you follow him?" Alice asked.

The poor girl hadn't even caught her breath yet, but she nodded. "Yes, mistress."

"And?"

"Marchley's Boardinghouse, my lady."

"Excellent."

She grabbed her cloak from her armoire and marched toward the door.

"My lady, no! You can't go there. Especially unaccompanied."

"I won't be unaccompanied. You're coming with me."

She was through the door and down the back stairs before Rose could say another word.

"Rosie, where have you been all morning?" Mrs. Branson, the housekeeper, called out from the parlor. "Come and give us a hand in here. Her ladyship has several guests coming, and that silly girl Peg is ill again."

"Go," Alice said. "I'll be fine."

"What? My lady, no—"

But Alice was out the door before Rose could say anything else.

Her driver was likewise unhappy with her orders but too used to obeying her to question her.

Her rush of excitement lasted until the carriage pulled to a stop in front of the boardinghouse. Her bravado ebbed with the imminent prospect of marching into such an establishment, on her own, to confront a man. *Alone.*

But she was desperate. And she wouldn't take no for an answer.

Alice took a deep breath and alighted from the carriage, ignoring her driver's protests. He might not approve, but she was reasonably sure he would keep her destination to himself. He was one of a handful of servants who felt more pity for her than loyalty to her mother, however afraid they might be to show it. Not that she blamed them. Honestly, she was rather shocked she'd gotten the man to drive her to the boardinghouse. If her mother found out, he'd be in a world of trouble. Another good reason for him to keep his mouth shut, though Alice would be sure to claim the man had no notion of what she was up to.

She marched into the establishment and straight up the stairs. Her confidence took another hit when she realized she had no idea which room was his. Asking the proprietor would be more brazen than she was ready to be. She'd worn the plainest dress she owned, but even that was too fine to blend in here. She might not care who saw her, but she wasn't so foolish as to go out of her way to announce her intention to enter the room of a man she wasn't related to, either.

She knew she'd been observed leaving the house, which meant she might not have a great deal of time. Alice had no doubt that one of Mother's spies had rushed off to tattle on her. It hardly mattered now. Mother had already done her worst. Alice's engagement to Lord Woolsmere would be announced shortly. And Philip was leaving. She didn't have any time to imagine all the potentially horrible outcomes to her actions. She knew what she wanted to do. And she needed Philip's help. End of story.

Alice stared at her choice of doors. Three were open, the rooms empty. Two had noises emanating from them. She didn't know whether to giggle or run from the building with her hands over her ears. That left the one at the end of the corridor and the one just to her right. No sound came from behind the door nearest her, so she stole as quietly as possible to the end of the corridor. Faint shuffling and rustlings could be heard and, before she could talk herself out of it, she knocked on the door. She gathered her skirts in her hands, prepared to run if anyone other than Philip opened the door.

The door swung open, revealing Philip's shocked face. Her face broke into a grin with the relief flooding through her.

"Let me in before someone sees me," she said, pushing her way past him.

He stared, dumbstruck. "Ye shouldna be here."

"I know. Bit of a moot point now, don't you think?"

He didn't respond, though his eyes narrowed.

"You might want to close the door before someone catches sight of me."

Philip still hesitated, clearly torn, before finally shutting the door. He paused for a moment, his eyes roaming over her, squinting in confusion. She half expected him to open the door again and toss her out. Instead, he snorted and turned his back, resuming what he'd been doing.

"Aren't you going to ask me why I'm here?" she asked, watching him pack his belongings with a precise and meticulous care that would surpass even Mrs. Branson's impossible standards.

"Dinna need to ask what I already ken. And it willna do ye any good."

"What won't?"

"I'm no' going to help ye run away. Ye'll simply have to stay and face yer responsibilities like a good lassie."

She sucked in a deep breath, trying to keep the rage that had been building in her chest for the last several weeks from boiling over. She needed Philip's help. Shrieking at him now would be the wrong way of going about getting it.

"You make me sound like a trained lap dog."

Philip shrugged. "If that's how ye choose to see it."

"How else am I supposed to take that statement?"

Philip sighed and paused in his packing. "A good lass

obeys her father. There's no shame in that. The man has been responsible for yer upkeep and well-being all yer life. And has done a fine job of it, too, from the looks of ye. Respect and obedience are the least ye owe him."

"So, because my father has provided for me, I'm supposed to let him dictate the rest of my life? Shackle me to a man who repulses me, who can do with me as he chooses, for the rest of my days? Which may very well be limited, if the rumors prove true?"

"Aye." Philip shrugged again. "It's the way of the world. Of your world, in any case. No sense in feigning surprise now."

"How is that fair?"

At that, he snorted out a laugh. "Whoever told ye life was supposed to be fair? And I'll tell ye another thing," he said, adding a pristinely folded shirt to his saddlebag. "Being wed to a wealthy man who will keep ye dripping in silks and baubles is a good sight more than a great many lasses can look forward to."

He looked her over again and shook his head. "You were bred to sit in salons and be waited on hand and foot. Ye wouldna last a week without yer palace full of comforts. *And* ye have a man willing to provide that for ye. Go home."

Alice crossed her arms, swallowing past the lump in her throat and the barrage of tears that threatened from her bottled-up emotions. "I realize I am a pampered, spoiled little princess who has never had to lift a finger for myself my whole life. There's not much I can do about that. But even a woman such as I deserve the chance to live unmolested and unafraid. I am not some weak, simpering little miss who will fall apart at the first sign of difficulty. I'm tired of people assuming I'm too delicate to live as I see fit. I'm going to take my life back. And you're going to help me."

Philip slowly shook his head, his face set in regretful,

albeit stubborn, lines. "Ye're mistaken, my lady."

A deadly calm filled her, mingled with a slight streak of guilt that she steadfastly ignored. "Oh no, I'm not. I'm going to leave this place. I'm going to find Elizabet. And you are going to help me. Or I will alert the authorities to your presence in the city. I will betray your identity as a member of the Highland Highwayman's gang of thieves."

Philip stared her down with an expression so full of anger and disdain that it took all her willpower not to flinch. "Do yer worst, my lady," he said, his voice all the more terrifying for its quietness. "I wasna exiled with John. I was arrested and released. I may not be particularly welcome in London, but I'm no' breaking any laws being here, either."

"Yes, because there was no evidence against you. But I have a letter," she said, pulling it partially from her bodice before tucking it back in. "From Elizabet, that she sent to me before she left. She refers to you as John MacGregor's man. Which is all your enemies will need to get you thrown into prison."

"Perhaps. Perhaps not," he said. "It may garner some interest, but it's scarcely enough to see me hanged."

"True," she said, taking a tremulous breath before she levied the true blackmail against him. "This may not send you to your death. But it will bring attention to you. Attention I assume you are eager to avoid."

Philip's expression turned thunderous, and Alice couldn't stop herself from taking a step backward this time.

"And ye call yerself Lady Elizabet's friend," he all but spat at her.

"I *am* her friend. I love her more dearly than anyone else."

"Yet ye'd threaten her safety by betraying me to Ramsay, all for the sake of saving yerself from a marriage most lasses would kill for."

"No! I'd never endanger Elizabet."

"Oh, aye? And what do ye think will happen if ye tell Ramsay I'm here? If he finds me, he'll stop at nothing to use me to find John and Elizabet."

Alice shook her head, the thought of Fergus Ramsay finding her friend sickening her. Fergus had been humiliated when Elizabet had run from him to be with John. And, according to Elizabet, the broken betrothal had also cost him her dowry estates, which he and Lord Dawsey, Elizabet's father, had been using as a base for their smuggling operations. While Elizabet had followed John into exile, she'd made certain to send a solicitor with the proper documents necessary to claim her inheritance once she and John had wed—effectively ruining her father's and Ramsay's plans for her property.

To say Ramsay was sore over the issue was an understatement. He wasn't exactly quiet about the retribution he'd like to exact if he ever got his hands on John again. And by extension, Elizabet. And knowing Ramsay, he'd be only too eager to personally make sure Elizabet suffered.

Alice would never do anything to hurt Elizabet. Which meant she would never follow through on her threats. But Philip didn't need to know that. She steeled her spine and raised her chin. She needed him to believe she was strong enough to do what she said. "Once I expose you as a highwayman, you won't be going anywhere but prison. There will be very little chance of danger to them. Ramsay won't be able to touch you."

"If ye believe that, lass, ye're more naive than I thought."

She straightened her shoulders, strengthening her resolve. She knew her threats were empty. Knew he was right. If there was even the possibility that Ramsay could get to Philip, and through him, to Elizabet and John, she wouldn't utter a peep. But she didn't need to actually betray him. He needed only to believe she would. Then they'd both be on their way out of the city, and no one would be the wiser until it was too late.

"Think of me what you will. I don't care for your opinion of me, only that you take me with you when you leave. The choice is yours. Take me to Elizabet. Or I betray your presence to the authorities. And anyone else who might wish to know."

Philip latched the flap of his saddlebag and dropped it on the floor. Yet still he said nothing. His fists clenched and unclenched by his side, his jaw visibly straining, as if he were trying to restrain himself. From speaking? From throttling her?

It mattered not. She didn't enjoy having to resort to blackmail. But if that's what it took to escape this marriage and the people controlling her, to take her life into her own hands for once, then so be it.

It took everything she had, but she waited silently while he made up his mind.

He finally spoke, though each word sounded as if he was forcing it from his throat. "Very well. I'll take ye to Scotland, but I'll no' take ye directly to John and Elizabet. It's too dangerous."

"I don't care about the danger."

"I do," he said, looming so close she had to take a step or fall over. "And they care a great deal about the danger to them. I care not about what danger ye may get yerself into."

Anger spiked through Alice, but she had scant cause for it. She *was* blackmailing the man, after all. She could hardly expect him to be happy about it.

"And what do I do once we reach Scotland?" she asked.

Philip shrugged. "Maybe ye can gain an audience with the Lion and his lady and plead yer case. If they feel like helping ye, so be it. I'll wash my hands of ye the moment we arrive."

Nervousness wormed its way through her, sending a chill through her veins and setting her stomach to twisting. She was really going to do this. Leave her home, her comforts, everything she'd ever known, for a chance to live life on her own terms. Even if to do that, she'd have to trust a man who hated her and had promised to bring her to a castle full of his kin who would probably feel the same way.

But it was worth it.

And once she found Elizabet, she'd come up with a solution to her mess of a life. Her own solution—*her* choices, her decisions. Elizabet would understand. She'd been in the same situation and had done the same thing. Minus the blackmail, she assumed.

She gave him a decisive nod. "Then we have a bargain."

"If ye wish to call it so."

She ignored that. "When do we leave?"

He gathered his saddlebags and threw them over his shoulder. "I am leaving right now."

"But…wait, I can't…"

"You," he said, "may leave whenever ye like. We canna be seen leaving the city together. I am bringing my laird and his lady some supplies they've requested. I take ship at Dover a week from today to travel up the coast to Scotland. If ye wish me to take ye, meet me there."

"How am I supposed to do that?" she asked, frowning.

"I dinna care. If ye want to go badly enough, ye'll find a way. But ye better be smart about it. Dinna tell anyone ye're going. Dinna let anyone see ye or follow ye. And dinna go spreading my name about. Get to Dover, undetected, and get passage on the ship. I'll meet ye on board. If ye're not there when the ship sets sail, I'll assume ye came to yer senses."

He threw open the door and marched out, not waiting for a response from her.

Alice sat on the bed, her legs suddenly trembling. She

hadn't expected to have to make her way anywhere on her own. That had been the whole point in blackmailing him. Although, she did understand his reasoning, even if it threw her plans into turmoil. If she was seen with him, it would be far too easy to both trace her to find Elizabet, and through her, the exiled John. Traveling openly with Philip was therefore out of the question, at least until they were out of London.

But that left her with the problem of getting to Dover, and onto that ship, alone.

She took a deep breath, squared her shoulders, and stood up. This was what she'd wanted. So she needed to be prepared to do what it took. And do it she would.

She couldn't wait to see Philip's face when he boarded the ship in Dover. Because she had every intention of not only making it there but getting there before him. Proving him wrong would be worth any hardship she had to endure.

Chapter Four

Philip handed the last box to the waiting sailor on the dock and then turned to William who climbed back into the wagon.

"That seems to be the last of it," Philip said, patting the horse's neck.

Young Will looked down at him. "Are ye sure ye dinna need anything else for the journey? The Lady Elizabet left quite a few belongings. I'm sure I could get her maid to retrieve a few more things."

"Nay. We dinna want to draw too much attention to ourselves. And we're already bringing more than they requested. Dinna forget, I'm going to have to find a way to transport all of this once we reach port."

Philip glanced around the bustling dock and then back at the young man sitting in the wagon, trying not to let his concern show on his face. He must not have been successful, though, because young William scowled.

"I'll be fine, Philip," he said. "I'm not the same green boy that I once was."

"I ken that well enough, lad. If I didna think ye could

handle yerself, I'd not send ye back to be our eyes and ears in Ramsay's ranks. But just because I trust ye doesna mean I'm happy with sending ye to spy on the devil himself." Philip patted the horse again, keeping his gaze on it rather than on the young man in front of him. Not only to protect William's sensibilities, but to try to keep his own emotions in check.

William had been with him for the last several years—riding raids with Philip and John, who was better known as the Highland Highwayman in these parts. But now that John was an outlaw in exile with the Lady Elizabet, the highwayman's crew had been disbanded. Most of the men had gone on to seek other employment, both legal and not so legal.

Philip had stayed around for a few months to garner what information he could on Fergus Campbell, or Ramsay, as he liked to call himself now. The man who was responsible for John's arrest and ultimate exile. William had managed to secure a position with Ramsay. A fact which both pleased and dismayed Philip. Pleased, because they desperately needed to keep an eye on Ramsay's activities. But dismayed because, while William was strong and loyal, he did tend to take more risks than Philip would like.

However, his position would afford them much needed information on Ramsay's plans. He had been quiet lately, but Philip had no doubt he was still after revenge on the MacGregors, who he blamed for his downfall in both his relations with his father and the king. And, thanks to John making off with Ramsay's intended bride, the failure of his criminal organization, as well.

While Lady Elizabet had been a willing hostage for her now husband, the story around court was that she had been kidnapped as an act of revenge against her father, the Earl of Dawsey, and Ramsay, who had been her betrothed, as they were the men who had orchestrated John's supposed downfall. To add insult to injury, Ramsay had also accused

John of kidnapping Elizabet as a way to collect dower lands through forced marriage, though that had been the true reason Ramsay himself had wanted to wed her. The real story, that Lady Elizabet had fallen madly in love with John and had not only willingly accompanied him but had shown up uninvited and unannounced in order to force him to take her with him, was not commonly known.

"I promise I'll be fine," William said, looking down at Philip with fond exasperation.

"Aye, ye will," Philip said with a smile. "I've trained ye well. But that doesna mean I willna worry. Are ye sure ye wouldna rather accompany me to Glenlyon? I could use yer help."

He knew it was unfair of him to play on the lad's sense of loyalty by pleading for help, but he would do more than that if it meant keeping the young man at his side. He truly had no doubt that William would do well, no matter what he chose to do. Still, he had much growing to do. Despite his training with John's men, he remained impetuous and headstrong. Those traits had gotten him into more than one scrape while riding with the highwaymen. A few more years under the wing of Philip and the men of Glenlyon would shape him into a fine warrior.

"Stop worrying so, Cousin," William said. "I ken where to find ye if I need ye. Ye're the one I'm worried about."

"And why is that?"

William smiled with a wicked twinkle in his eye. "Lady Alice doesna seem the type to give up so easily."

Philip snorted. "Aye. Lady Elizabet's adventures seem to have put the ridiculous notion in Lady Alice's head that running away with outlaws is the best way to escape an unwanted marriage."

"And telling her otherwise didna work so well, I take it, since ye've not stopped watching the roads for her since we arrived."

Philip shook his head. "I'd have better luck talking to the stone wall in the castle privy."

William laughed, though he, too, kept searching the road. "Perhaps yer words made a dent, after all. It doesna look as if the lady is coming."

"Canna say I'm surprised," Philip said with a half smile. "I've no doubt she tried. She seems a thick-heided goat, that one. But the lady was daft to think she'd be able to make it one day away from her pampered existence. Let alone navigate the road to Dover by herself. Still, we canna be too careful of Ramsay's men. He'd do anything to get to John and the Lady Elizabet. And he ken's well enough how she felt about Lady Alice. I've no doubt she's been watched, which means there's a good chance he's seen my face, as well. Take care, laddie. Careful or no, we may have been spotted together by someone who'd report it."

"Dinna fash, Cousin. I'll be well."

A bell sounded on the ship, and a sailor hollered down the gangplank to him.

"You'd best board, sir, if you're coming!"

"On my way." Philip turned to look at Will one last time and gave his thigh a pat. "Godspeed to ye then, young William."

"And to you, Cousin."

Philip nodded and hurried up the gangplank just as the sailors pulled it aboard. He stood at the deck and waved goodbye to William as the shore slowly receded. He'd miss the young lad. He hoped he'd see him a few months hence at the yearly Gathering at Glenlyon, but Will had been at his side for many years. Being without him would be odd.

Philip turned to one of the sailors hurrying by. "Have my belongings been brought to my cabin?"

"Aye, sir. Everything has been delivered. And your sister

has already been settled as well."

Philip stopped so suddenly the sailor almost ran into him. He turned, his eyes wide and his stomach sinking into his knees.

"My sister?"

. . .

The cabin door crashed open, and Alice jumped back against the bunk with a shriek. She sucked in a deep breath at the sight of the wild-eyed Scot staring at her from the doorway.

"What the devil are ye doing here?" he asked, his expression somewhere between furious and scandalized.

She forced her breathing to slow and drew herself up to her full height to face him. "What do you mean, what am I doing here? You said to meet you on the ship at Dover. I did exactly as you asked."

"Aye but…"

"But what?" Alice put her hands on her hips and glared at him. "I followed your directions to the letter. You told me if I could get here, you would take me to Elizabet. Well, I'm here. Are you a man of your word or not?"

His eyes narrowed. "I've always been a man of my word. But I didna think…"

"You didn't think what? That I'd actually be able to get here? You assumed that you'd found a way out of our agreement, and now that I've managed to do what you asked, what…you'll go back on your word?"

He visibly struggled to control his temper. She crossed her arms and waited for an answer, refusing to cower before the angry warrior. They had a bargain, and she was going to make sure he held up his end.

"Ye have no business here and ye know it. 'Tis a long journey, and that bastard Ramsay is still searching for my laird. As ye're friends with his lady, there's no doubt that the scoundrel has been keeping an eye on ye. Ye've probably led him right to us."

"If that were the case, then he'd be standing in this cabin. But as he's not, I think we're safe. I am not so stupid as all that. I took every precaution to ensure that no one followed me."

"How the devil did ye get here?"

Alice gave him a smile she knew held more than a little smugness. "I convinced my father that I needed a holiday, some time away to gather myself and prepare for the coming engagement."

"And he chose Dover?"

"We are supposed to set sail for Calais in the morning."

"And when no one can find ye, what do ye think will happen then? The entire town will be up in arms to find ye. Exactly the kind of attention we dinna want."

She released an exasperated sigh. "Only Rose, my maid, knows I've left, and I trust her with my life. I undertook all my preparations in secret, Rose took care of all the arrangements, and as far as my family knows, I am out buying a new hat to wear on the ship, after which Rose will explain that I am overtired and gone to bed early. No one will be the wiser until they are ready to board the ship. Or even longer, if Rose can convince them I went ahead. Meaning, we should be quite safe with at least a day's lead before anyone knows I am not where I should be."

Philip frowned. "So you hope! Ye canna know for sure all will go to plan. If ye had stayed put, there'd be no danger at all. No one notices my comings or goings. But you? Lord Morley's daughter, by all that is holy. All it takes is for a maid to open your empty bedroom door and all hell will break loose."

Alice glared at him, anger coursing through her. That

the anger stemmed both from his unfair accusations and the fear he might be right, she ignored. "There is no reason to assume my plan will not work. My parents go for days without seeing me. And with my mood of late, I can promise you they won't be seeking my company. And for someone who is so concerned over strangers knowing your business, you are certainly shouting it loudly enough with the door wide open."

Philip blinked at her, opened his mouth to argue, and promptly shut it again. He stepped close enough that he could speak in a deep, low voice that reverberated through her chest but was quiet enough not to draw attention from anyone else. "Aye, I'll keep my voice down. But I'll no' completely destroy yer reputation by shutting ye in alone with me. This isna the boardinghouse, though that was bad enough. There is nowhere to hide here and no way to leave unseen. If ye have no thought for yer future, ye should be thankful I do."

She straightened her spine, refusing to back down. "Of course I have a thought for my future. I wouldn't be here at all if I hadn't a care for that. And while I have serious doubts that anyone other than you cares in which cabin I sleep, I did let it be known that I am your sister, remember? Therefore, any interaction between us is perfectly natural, and being alone with me shouldn't present any problems. In fact, it is to be expected. So as long as you can hold your temper, my presence shouldn't draw any untoward attention."

He closed his eyes briefly and took a deep breath. "Will ye no' see reason?" he said again. "Ye're only putting my laird and his lady at risk."

"No more so than you," she said. "And probably a great deal less. Has it not occurred to you that my presence at Elizabet's side could help her? Ramsay wouldn't dare attack me. My father would bury him. Besides, if Ramsay is having me watched, don't you think that he also has Elizabet's home watched? Her own father is one of the people she is hiding from. Yet you went to her home to collect her belongings."

"I went in secret and spoke to no one but her trusted maid, the one who helped her escape and who she trusts implicitly. I also took every precaution to ensure that I wasna followed either throughout town or on my way here."

"And I did the same. Is it so hard to believe that I could be capable of subterfuge?"

"Hard to believe? With ye standing there looking smug as a cat in the cream? Nay, lady, I have no doubt as to yer talent for subterfuge."

Alice swallowed hard, surprised at how much that stung. She'd asked the question, but he was the one who'd turned it into an insult. But she'd never let him know that he'd hurt her with his careless words.

"I did as you directed. So I ask again. Are you going to keep your word and take me to Elizabet or not?"

The vein on his forehead showed briefly, and she could almost hear his teeth grinding. She had to admire his obvious restraint, even if the reason for it was totally unfounded. He muttered something about the saints and needing to be saved before he spoke again.

"Ye canna stay here in this cabin with me. Even being in it now could ruin ye if you're recognized. Why did ye not ask for yer own accommodations?"

"Who is going to recognize me? No one I am acquainted with would set foot in Scotland. And besides, I did," she said with a slight shrug. "There were no other accommodations to be had. This ship has but a few passenger cabins, and they are all booked. I had no choice but to tell the captain that we were traveling together. Besides, as you are so concerned for my safety, it is much better for the crew to believe that I am your sister rather than a woman on her own."

He stepped closer, so close the heat from his body warmed hers.

"I am little better than a stranger to ye," he said, and the sudden predatory look in his eyes made her stomach drop down to her toes. A not altogether unpleasant sensation, although it did serve to remind her that he was right. She didn't know him. Yet. What she knew of him through their brief acquaintance and through Elizabet told her he could be trusted. Still, she had to steel herself not to step back.

"No matter what others may think, ye're no kin of mine. Ye're a bonnie lass. The bonniest I've seen in a good long while. Did ye not consider what ye might be risking sharing my cabin?"

His eyes roamed over her, and he let her see exactly how much he enjoyed what he saw. She knew he was merely trying to frighten her. Or, at the very least, make her rethink her plans. But it wouldn't work. Despite the fine tremor that ran through her.

The slow smile he gave her would probably invade her dreams for the rest of her days.

"The heat staining yer cheeks betrays ye," he said, the gentleness of the finger he drew down her face contrasting with the gravelly deepness of his voice. "Do ye no' consider me a man then? That I wouldna be tempted by a beautiful woman in such close quarters?"

She swallowed and dragged enough air into her suddenly tortured lungs so she could speak. "You've had ample opportunity to seduce me, Mr. MacGregor. Had you wished, you would have done so back at the inn."

"Perhaps," he said, his hand cupping her face before dropping to trail down her neck. "Regardless...you being here now...presents quite a few problems I'd hoped to avoid."

So, the big, bad warrior found her presence problematic? She'd always heard Highlanders were lusting, ravaging beasts. She'd started to have her doubts, but maybe the lustful bit wasn't too far off the mark. She hoped. He would be the perfect diversion. Everything she needed. And she'd keep telling herself that until her knees stopped quaking and her heart beat calmly in her chest.

Alice straightened her shoulders. Two could play this game. She moved closer, crowding him until he had to back up or let her press herself against him. He did not back up. "I'd call them opportunities. Not problems."

She drew a finger down his chest, her heart thundering at her temerity. But she had nothing to lose at this point. She'd left her home, willingly put herself in this man's hands. And after the small taste she'd gotten the other night, there was no place she'd rather be. Despite his glaring eyes, the heart beneath her hand thundered in time with her own. The urge to find out how far the heat building in her could go before consuming her was almost unbearable. She tried to ignore the hint of fear ricocheting in her belly at what, for all her bravado, she knew very little about.

Truthfully, she hadn't thought much about what might happen if he took her up on any of her invitations. She was drawn to him like she'd never been to another man, and she enjoyed flirting. That Philip was obviously not the flirting type hadn't mattered much. It was fun. It suited her purposes, and she could be honest enough with herself to admit she rarely bothered to rein in her impulses. But she was beginning to realize that she should be more cautious when it came to the brooding Highlander standing before her. He didn't play the same game as the chivalrous courtiers to whom she was accustomed. The courtly boundaries followed by most would mean nothing to him.

On the one hand, he was handsome to a distraction, with a body that was made for vigorous physical activity. She already knew what the slightest brush of his lips did to her. The thought of him employing all the weapons in his generous armament was nearly more than she could bear—

quickly becoming a thirst she would do anything to quench. But on the other hand, he might be the fire that finally burned her beyond saving. He was unlike any man she'd ever known. She'd be a fool to treat him as anything less.

He caught her hand and shook his head. But he didn't release her.

"Dinna push me too far, lass. Even a man of honor has a breaking point."

"I hope so," she said, changing the trepidation in her voice into what she hoped was an alluring purr.

He stepped away from her and shook his head. "Ye dinna ken what ye ask. Someday ye'll thank me for my restraint."

So says he. Maybe he was right. But it was hard to keep that in mind when her body craved his touch. And he could bluster all he wanted. She could tell he liked having her in his arms. She'd just have to make him admit that.

Chapter Five

Before Alice could say anything, a sharp gasp echoed down the hallway. Philip spun to see who was there while Alice craned her neck around his bulk to do the same. In the hallway stood a vicar accompanying two women. The older and more pious-looking one had her arm wrapped around the slim shoulders of a young girl who peered at Alice with interest.

"You're Scottish," she said, prompting the older woman to clutch the girl tighter and stare at Philip with abject fear.

Alice resisted the urge to roll her eyes. Instead she put on her brightest smile and bent down until she was eye level with the child. "Aye, that we are," she said, with a decent Scottish brogue, if she did say so herself. "That's my brother." She jerked her thumb at him. "Dinna mind him. He's a great, hulking beast, but gentle as a lamb." She winked, and the child gave her a shy smile.

"Your brother, eh?" the woman said. "You don't resemble each other at all."

"Well aren't ye kind," Alice said, aiming a pleased smile

at the woman, though she'd rather have pushed the busybody out the door. "A worse fate than being his spitting image I canna imagine. I do take after my mother, so I've been told."

The woman and the vicar gave them a speculative glance, but they must have passed muster because the woman gave them a curt head bob and then hustled the girl back down the corridor. The vicar didn't seem as convinced.

For all her boldness, Alice couldn't help the sinking feeling in her stomach that years of her mother's upbringing forced on her. She wouldn't turn back, but Philip hadn't been exaggerating when he pointed out how dangerous this trip was not only for her life but for her reputation. If she was unable to get to Elizabet and had to return home, no man would have her now. That the whole reason she was on the ship in the first place was to get away from marriage didn't elude her. But she did want to marry someday. Just not the ancient, controlling, and possibly murderous earl her parents had chosen. Which meant that she needed to make it to Elizabet with her reputation intact. However, if she had to sacrifice it for the sake of her freedom, she would. There were worse things than being a disgraced spinster. Like being a dead wife. Or worse, an oppressed, captive one.

The vicar stood glancing between them, his hands clasped in front of him.

"I apologize for my sister's outburst," he said. "I am sure there is nothing untoward going on."

"Och, look at that, brother dear," Alice said to Philip. "Another brother accompanying his sister on a journey. Isn't that grand?"

She glanced at Philip, whose lips were pressed into a thin line while his nostrils flared slightly. If he was anything like her, he was resisting the urge to tell the vicar exactly whose business it was. Namely not his. However, the woman in the hallway had seemed more than ready to make a scene. And

Alice wasn't so sure the vicar wouldn't make matters worse. Sailors had their superstitions. The presence of women wasn't always welcome, a single woman especially. They might tolerate it, but they weren't always happy with the situation. And the captain might be hard-pressed to keep the peace if anyone decided to make a stink about their situation.

She smiled sweetly at the vicar, putting her eyelashes to good use. He may be a man of the cloth, but Alice had found little difference between clergymen and any other male when it came to the fairer sex.

"Is everything all right?" the vicar asked. "I thought I heard raised voices."

"There is no issue here," she said. "Simply a minor misunderstanding with my brother."

"I see. Is there anything I may do to help?"

Philip drew himself up to his considerable height, dwarfing the man beside him.

"No, thank ye, Reverend," Philip said, his tone both warning and menacing. "The...my...sister will be disembarking shortly."

The vicar frowned. "I don't see how that is possible, sir. We have long since passed the shore and, with the wind in our sails and the current with us, I do not think it possible for the captain to return, even if he were so inclined."

Alice grinned in triumph, and Philip glared at her.

"Are you sure everything is all right?" the vicar asked again.

"Of course," Alice said. "My brother is put out that my belongings are taking up so much space." She pointed to the large trunk sitting near the bunk.

"Ah, I see," he said, with an indulgent smile. "I suppose ladies are wont to travel heavily, aren't they? Well, perhaps other accommodations may be found for the lady?" he asked, glancing at Philip.

"There are no other accommodations to be had," Alice said. "But no worries. We will make do with the space provided. Hopefully, the weather will hold and the journey will be quick. And then my brother can deposit me at my destination and be quit of me." She infused her words with as much good-natured humor as she could muster, and even threw in a wink for the vicar, who chuckled and waved goodbye as he turned back up the corridor. But she'd meant every word.

"Now ye've done it," Philip all but growled at her. He shut the door and marched back to her. "Ye've stuck us with each other for the duration of the journey and lied to a man of God on top of it."

Alice glanced at him, eyebrow raised. "Does a lie to a clergyman matter so much more than any other lie?"

"Aye, a lie to a man of God might carry a bit more weight."

"Well, that seems unfair. A lie is a lie, I say."

"Aye! Aye, I say it too. Ye shouldna ha' lied. At all. To anyone."

She waved away his concern. "It was but a small untruth."

"Small?"

"We're traveling together, staying in the same quarters, journeying to the same destination. The only untruth is our blood relation. A small thing if you consider that the rest of what we told him was true."

That vein in his forehead throbbed again and, if he kept grinding his teeth every time they spoke, he wouldn't have any left by the time they reached Scotland. She bit her lip to keep from smiling. She did tend to have that effect on people. Especially people who were trying to get her to do something she didn't want to do. Stubborn, Elizabet used to call it.

"And why did ye speak with an accent?" he finally managed to grind out. "A horrible one, at that."

"It wasn't so bad. Besides," she shrugged, "I'm supposed

to be your sister. It would be odd if we didn't sound alike."

He released a long-suffering sigh. "Ye could have said ye were my half sister, or that I'd been fostered abroad, or any number of other lies that would have explained your lack of accent. Or, ye could have said nothing."

She opened her mouth to argue but then closed it again with a little laugh. "I suppose it's something I would have questioned, so I assumed others would as well."

"Aye, well most people are too polite to question strangers about their manner of speech, even if they find it odd."

Her mouth did drop open at that. "Are you saying I'm rude?"

"I've called ye a great many things since we met and *this* is the one ye take offense to?"

"Absolutely. I try never to be rude."

Philip closed his eyes and rubbed his hand over his face. He took a deep, fortifying breath before opening his eyes to look at her again. Her father often did the same thing during their conversations. Alice wondered if he'd like to know that he wasn't the only one whose patience she tested. Thinking of her father gave her a small pang of homesickness. He'd been a good father to her, aside from the small matter of trying to wed her to a man who would likely kill her when she couldn't bear his heir. Though, even there, she knew her father had her best interests in mind. Or at least he thought he did. He'd found a man with wealth and social stature, a man who, on paper, was an ideal match. In her father's mind at least, since he put no stock in what he called idle gossip.

But her father wasn't the one who'd have to lie in bed enduring the man's clammy-handed touch. Or who'd have to sleep next to a man who might murder her before morning. He wouldn't spend his life always looking over his shoulder, being afraid to eat or drink anything put in front of him. The earl had already buried *several* wives. Their manner of deaths might be in dispute, but their demises weren't. Being the next in line was enough to frighten anyone. So, good intentions or not, she'd done what she'd had to do.

"Listen," she said, but Philip raised a finger to stop her. She folded her arms and tried again. "I was simply—"

He raised his finger again and then pointed at her as if he'd berate her like a scolding nursemaid. He looked like he was going to speak several times. Then he shook his head, clapped his hat on, and strode to the door. She made to follow, but he turned on her before she could.

"If we're to be stuck together in this box for the duration of the journey, shove that trunk somewhere out of the way so we can walk about without tripping. Ye'll sleep on the top bunk," he said, jabbing a finger in that direction, "and ye'll keep yerself suitably covered at all times."

She folded her arms again. "Anything else?"

"Aye, stay put. I dinna want ye wandering about getting up to God knows what."

He turned on his heel and left.

Alice watched, pleased, as he stalked down the corridor. He seemed to have accepted their travel arrangements. But if he thought he could order her about, he needed to think again. Her real relatives had been trying to get her to obey for years. She hadn't escaped their tyranny to follow someone else's orders. Her life was hers now.

Poor Philip didn't know what he was in for.

• • •

He stayed away for as long as he deemed safe. As much as he wanted to put some distance between him and his persistent travel companion, he didn't want to leave her to her own devices too long. No good could come of that.

When he returned to the cabin, he was pleased to see her

trunk was no longer in the middle of the floor. Until he saw where she'd moved it.

"Ye canna put yer things there," he said, pointing to his former bunk that was now occupied by two travel bags, the contents of one trunk, and a very bored Alice.

She held up a finger, her lips moving silently as she stared at a spot beyond his head.

He crossed his arms and waited for her to acknowledge him.

She squinted slightly and then sat back with a sigh. "Three hundred and twenty-eight."

He raised an eyebrow.

"There are three hundred and twenty-eight dark spots in the wood of that wall," she said, pointing to it. "Two hundred and eighteen on that one," she said, pointing to the one that held the single, small window. "I haven't checked this one yet," she said, gesturing to the wall next to the bunk. "But the light isn't very good, so I'll probably miss some."

"As long as it keeps ye busy," he said, not joking, despite his dry tone. She could count all the wood spots she wanted as long as she stayed out of trouble.

She glanced at him, her eyes narrowing slightly. He'd have thought she was glaring except the glazed look in her eye suggested she still wasn't focused on him. Perhaps she'd gone partially blind from sheer boredom.

He turned his attention back to the bigger problem at hand. "Why the devil did ye cover my bunk with yer belongings?"

She shrugged. "It was too heavy to push beneath the bunk with everything in it, and you did tell me to get it out of the way so we could move about." She spread her hands out. "There is no longer anything on the floor to hamper our movements."

He blew a breath out through his nose in an effort to

both stem his growing aggravation and squash the hint of amusement that threatened to erupt. God, she was a cheeky thing.

"And where do ye propose I sleep?"

She blinked innocently at him. "I wouldn't presume to make such a choice for you. However, the floor *is* now free and clear as instructed. Perhaps you could sleep there."

He narrowed his eyes at her. This would be the longest three-day voyage he'd ever had the displeasure of enduring.

Instead of giving her the courtesy of a response, he grabbed the trunk and her bags and stacked them against the far wall. Making *her* do it would have brought him considerably more satisfaction, but he didn't have the time or patience. He'd have to learn to pick his battles.

He grabbed an armload of dresses and underthings that were strewn on the bunk but couldn't bring himself to toss them in the trunk. Instead, he shook out each item before carefully folding them and putting them away. He didn't realize he'd settled into the soothing rhythm that he often sank into when performing such tasks until she spoke.

"What are you doing?"

He straightened. "Putting yer things away."

"But why?"

He frowned at that. "Because they were everywhere and ye didna seem inclined to do it."

Her forehead crinkled in confusion. "Yes, but…"

"I prefer my surroundings to be in order. Making ye clean up after yerself would ha' taken more energy than I've got at the moment."

She grimaced at that but begrudgingly thanked him with a quick glance in the trunk. "You do good work. Perhaps you could replace my maid, since I had to leave her behind."

He snorted and ignored that suggestion. "I'm afraid there's no' much in the way of entertainment on board. I ken what a hardship that will be for ye. I'd be happy to inform the captain that ye'll be disembarking at the next port, if ye feel it will be too great to endure."

She glared at him again, and he gave her his sweetest smile, which, he saw with a twinge of pleasure, flustered her. If she was determined to drive him mad with her flirtatious ways, he'd return the favor by being as obtuse as possible. And as a bonus, their squabbling would cement their pretense of being siblings. Most siblings he knew spent half their lives at each other's throats. He supposed he should be grateful she hadn't said they were married. Frankly, if they had to spend their lives together, one of them would probably be dead by the other's hand long before old age took them. It'd be a miracle if they made it off the boat in one piece.

"I shall endure the boredom as I must," she said. "It is a small price to pay to be safe from that murderous lecher Woolsmere and be reunited with my dear friend."

He shrugged. "Should ye change yer mind, I'll be happy to accommodate a request to return ye to yer home."

"Duly noted." She stood and smoothed down her skirts. "Well, then. If there is nothing else to keep us occupied in this tiny, dank chamber," she said with a pointed look at him, "then I suppose I shall wander above deck for a while."

She tried to push past him into the hallway, but he stopped her, swearing under his breath when she tried to pull away. "Ye canna go traipsing about on deck unaccompanied."

"I don't see why not," she said. "I traipsed onto the deck unaccompanied when I arrived and made it through sound enough."

"Because," he said, willing himself to be patient. "A ship full of sailors isna the safest of places for a bonnie lassie to be alone."

She turned to him with a brilliant smile that warmed him down to his toes. "You think I'm bonnie?"

She laughed when he scowled, which made him glower more. "Aye, ye're bonnie enough. But daft, reckless, and far too accustomed to getting yer own way."

"The last one, I'll give you, but what you call reckless, I call adventurous. And the daft remark I won't dignify with a response."

He chuckled, enjoying her company, despite himself.

"You can't keep me locked up in here," she said.

"I most certainly can. As yer supposed kinsmen, I can do whatever I choose with ye and none would tell me otherwise. But I'm no' so cruel as all that. Most of the time."

She arched an eyebrow at him, and his lips twitched into a reluctant smile. "I will take ye for air on the deck when I deem it safe and reasonable."

She dropped onto the bunk with a huff. "Safe and reasonable? You're worse than my father."

He gave her a wide grin at that remark. "Aye. And I care a great deal less for yer happiness than he, I'd wager. So as I said, the moment ye wish to return to yer obviously better suited circumstances, ye have only to ask."

He gave her a gallant bow and then pulled the door open. "I have a few more things to see to on deck. Ye'll stay put."

"But you just returned!"

"Aye. I thought it might be a good idea to make sure ye'd stayed where I left ye, since ye seem to have a habit of sneaking off."

She stood, arms crossed and dander up. "That is completely unfair. If you're going up on deck, there is no reason I shouldn't be able to go as well."

"Of course there is. I dinna wish to take ye."

He closed the door on her thunderous face with a chuckle that turned to a full-blown laugh when something solid hit the door behind him. He had no wish to have her along for the journey, but he couldn't deny she made it more interesting.

Philip lasted a mere seven minutes on deck before he sighed and turned back around to fetch her. She was right. He couldn't keep her locked up the whole time. Well, he could. But he'd never been unnecessarily cruel to anyone, and he probably shouldn't start with a lady. The weather was turning foul, but a few moments on deck should be fine if they stayed close to the entrance to the lower decks, in case they needed to get below quickly.

He opened the door to their cabin and slammed it shut again with a curse. The damned, blasted woman was nowhere to be seen. She must have left nearly the moment he had... and gone the other way, as he certainly hadn't seen her on his end.

He spun on his heel and hurried back on deck. The wind was already howling harder than a few moments ago, and he fought down the unease that settled like lead in his belly. He may have been purposely irking her before, but there was truth behind his words. She was safer below. Why couldn't she do as she was told?

The wind whipped his hair across his cheek, and he shoved it aside, his eyes scanning the deck. He expected her to be making her way back to the cabin. No sane woman would wish to stand about in such wind with rain on the horizon. Then again, nothing she did pointed much in the favor of sanity.

The crew scurried about, securing cargo and preparing for the coming storm. This late in the season, it probably wouldn't be too bad. But it didn't take much for circumstances to change. Most of the crew he asked hadn't seen Alice, but one man finally pointed him in the right direction.

He found her toward the bow of the ship, her eyes closed and her face upturned. The bolt of fear that spiked through him at seeing her, hair and skirts billowing out, standing against the backdrop of the foreboding sea, made his words much harsher than he intended.

"What are ye doing, ye daft woman? Ye'll blow overboard!"

"Doubtful," she said, taking a deep breath and then releasing it with a smile. "It's not so bad as all that. I needed some fresh air. And, since you refused to provide it..." She shrugged and turned her face into the wind again, sucking in another lungful. "Invigorating, isn't it?"

"Oh, aye. Until an extra strong gust whips ye right o'er the edge."

She rolled her eyes. "You worry too much. I would have gone below within good time."

"And when would that be? After ye'd been tossed into the deep? I'm no' following ye down there, just so ye ken."

She sighed and turned to head back to the other side of the ship. "It really isn't necessary to be such a miserable spoilsport, you know."

It probably wasn't. But watching her eyes flash when she was annoyed was something he found much more enjoyable than he should. However, now they had a genuine safety concern to deal with. And her refusal to understand the risks infuriated him.

Thunder cracked and the sky split, dropping heavy, fat drops on their heads. Alice gasped and flung her hands over her head in a futile attempt to keep herself dry.

He grabbed her arm and drew her to his side, trying to shield her with his bulk. The silly woman wasn't even wearing a cloak and, as he was in breeches rather than his much more useful kilt, both of them were soaked within seconds.

His sigh came out as more of a growl, and she looked up at him, eyes narrowed. "I havena made any secret of the fact that I'm no' happy with our situation, but no matter how we arrived at it, I agreed to take ye to Scotland, and I'll keep my word. Which places ye under my protection. I'm honor bound to ensure no harm comes to ye." At least until he could find a way to send her back to her family where she belonged, though he didn't think it prudent to share that with her.

"That includes making sure ye dinna drown because you're trying to prove yer independence. Aye?"

"Aye," she snapped back, trying to put as much space as possible between them while still staying in the shelter of his arms. "You've made yourself very clear."

"Good!"

The ship lurched beneath the strengthening waves, and she was thrown against him. She gasped and held tight. He held on to her much longer than was necessary to steady her. And he kept hold of her arm even then, though he glared down at her. He truly was being a surly bastard. But she unsettled him. Had turned his life upside down. He couldn't forgive that easily.

She didn't put up with his glowering for long. When it became clear he had no intention of releasing her, she wrenched her arm from his grasp and attempted to march back toward the short staircase that led below. Though with the ship rocking to and fro and the deck slick with rain, her grand escape resembled something more akin to a toddler taking her first steps than an elegant lady making an impressively sweeping exit.

He paused barely long enough to take a deep breath of air, and then followed her below. They would have to come up with some sort of an understanding. Or they'd never survive the trip.

Chapter Six

Alice staggered back into their cabin, using the walls on either side of her as aids for staying upright. Fury ate through her at Philip's overbearing ways. Yes, the weather had taken a turn for the worse. And had he given her another few seconds, she would have come back down on her own. But once he'd shown up, blustering and demanding, well, she'd had to draw out her excursion. Stand her ground. Let him know that she was not some country miss to be manhandled and ordered about. All it had gotten her was soaked through to the bone, but at least she'd asserted her independence.

She snorted at that thought, fully aware she was being unreasonable but too frustrated to care. It seemed there was no escape from controlling, know-it-all men, no matter how far she ran.

Philip was right on her heels, though he seemed to be handling the tossing ship with greater ease than she. He'd widened his stance to the point it should look ridiculous. But, as he was able to traverse the boards of the ship with merely a slight lurch here and there, and she was being tossed about like an empty flour sack, perhaps she should follow suit.

He entered the cabin behind her, and the door swung shut of its own volition. He had obviously not finished with her yet, but she had no intention of being berated like a child for something so ridiculous.

"I don't know why you are so angry with me," she said, reaching out to hold onto one of the bunks. "I wasn't up there longer than a few minutes. There were plenty of crewmen about."

"Ye think I trust yer protection to a ship-full of ruffians?"

She rolled her eyes at that. "To be honest, I didn't think you cared all that much about my protection."

The outrage on his face would have been comical except she could tell she'd truly offended him. She bit back the urge to apologize. She hadn't meant to malign his honor, but the man was insufferable.

He opened his mouth to speak, but she cut him off. "The captain couldn't very well continue to take passengers if his crew was in the habit of accosting them."

He couldn't argue with that, though she could see he wanted to. Before she could say anything else the ship tossed again and sent her flying into his arms. He caught her with a grunt. She tried to push away, but he held on tight.

"I'll be fine on my own," she said.

"Oh, I can see that." His chuckle reverberated through her chest.

"Let go." She pushed away from him, though it had more to do with the fine tingle running across her skin at his touch than her desire to put distance between them. In fact, what she truly wanted was to stay right where she was. And under normal circumstances she would have followed that impulse. But she was too irritated with him to give him the satisfaction.

"I left ye out of my sight for all of seven minutes and there ye were, soaking wet and shivering, and seconds from being tossed overboard. Oh aye, ye've proved ye can take care of yerself, all right."

"You left."

"I returned almost immediately. Ye couldna be patient."

She opened her mouth to argue but snapped it shut again, unfortunately unable to refute that.

"And, since ye couldna be patient *or* sensible, ye've proved ye canna be trusted."

She scowled at him. "You cannot keep me locked in this tiny box for the whole trip," she said.

He shrugged. "It's not that long of a journey."

She tried to put her hands on her hips to glare at him but the tilting ship made that impossible. If she didn't hang onto the bunk, she was going to go flying again. But she stared him down long enough that he finally let out an exasperated sigh.

"My offer still stands. I dinna want ye wondering about the ship on yer own. However," he said, holding up a finger to stave off her argument, "I agreed to accompany ye anywhere ye'd like to go, and I will keep my word."

She raised an eyebrow at him. "Well, that's very generous of you."

He snorted. "I'd rather be a nursemaid than have to explain to yer father why ye'd been defiled by a seaman or fell to the bottom of the ocean."

"I take it back," she said.

"Oh? I'm no' generous now?"

"No."

"Then what am I?" The half grin on his lips and the gleam in his eyes set her stomach roiling. Though perhaps that was merely the motion of the ship. He bit his lip and her knees nearly gave out. Not the ship. Though the incessant tossing of the waves wasn't helping matters.

"You're stubborn and cruel and selfish and pigheaded and…"

"I believe stubborn and pigheaded mean the same thing," he said, his grin widening.

She rolled her eyes. "And rude and coarse and…and…"

He'd been taking small steps toward her with every word, and now he stood a mere few inches away.

"Aye? What else am I?" His voice was as deep and rough as the storm-tossed sea outside and affected her as much. Even if she stood on solid ground, his voice would knock her off-kilter.

"You are…" She stopped and swallowed hard.

He was overwhelming, that's what he was. Exciting and dangerous. Mouthwateringly handsome. Potentially devastating. But she wasn't going to tell him that.

"You are…large," she finally said.

His laugh echoed throughout the cabin, and her own lips twitched into a smile. But before she could say anything more the ship lurched again, throwing her into the bunk. Her head banged on the edge of the wood, and pain shot through her skull. She cried out and put her hand to her head. It came away wet and sticky. She glanced up, her eyes wide. She knew her head was hurt, of course. But the pain she was experiencing didn't seem to warrant the amount of blood that gushed down her face.

Philip paled slightly, but he didn't hesitate. He dropped to his knees in front of her and grabbed a cloth from the small table by the bunk. He dabbed gently at her head. Then he placed the towel against her wound and pressed hard. She sucked in a breath but didn't fight him.

"Shh," he said, his voice surprisingly soothing. "It's no' so bad as all that."

"I'm not complaining."

He gave her a small but warm smile. "No, ye're not."

"You sound surprised."

"I am a bit."

Her eyes narrowed. "And why is that? Have the other ladies you've known been so delicate?"

He opened his mouth to answer and then gave her another smile. She steeled her stomach against the now-familiar flip his crooked grin caused.

"No," he said. "Actually, quite the opposite."

"Am I so different from them then?" She held her breath, waiting for the answer. The fondness in his eyes when he'd answered told her he admired the ladies in his life. That she wouldn't be the type of woman he would look upon with admiration stung more than she wanted to admit.

He didn't answer for a moment but instead looked at her, his eyes roaming over her face before stopping to stare into her eyes. "No," he said again. "Ye're no' so different at all. You're strong like them. And intelligent. Bonnie." He grinned again, and her heart skipped a few beats.

"You still think I'm bonnie? Even dripping wet and covered in blood?" she asked. She hated the weakness behind the question but couldn't help it. She wanted to hear him confirm it. Wanted to know he found her attractive.

"Aye," he said, lightly stroking her cheek.

He dabbed at her forehead again, but she barely felt the sting as that one soft word flowed through her like a soothing wave.

His eyes searched hers for a moment. He moved infinitesimally closer. Her breath caught in her throat, and she bit the corner of her lip. He was close enough to kiss. All she had to do was lean the slightest bit forward. And for a moment, she was certain that was what he wanted.

But then he sat back and continued with his description. "Bonnie, aye. But stubborn, shrewish, pigheaded..."

She arched an eyebrow at him. "Is that what you truly think? Or is it simply easier to throw my own insults back at me?"

His eyebrow quirked up. "Perhaps it's both."

He leaned forward to peer at her forehead, and her eyes closed. She breathed him in, reveled in the heat that seemed to seep into her very bones, though he barely touched her.

"There now," he said, giving her head one last dab before putting the cloth down. "I think ye'll do."

"Thank you," she murmured, forcing herself to meet his eyes. His breath danced across her mouth, and she bit her lip again, anything to keep from closing the distance between them. She expected him to move away, yet still he didn't. His gaze shifted to her mouth, and she could hear the hitch in his breath. He wasn't so unaffected by her as he liked to pretend. The knowledge burned through her with a triumphant passion. He wanted her. Whether he liked it or not.

He placed a hand on either side of her and she hoped he'd give in. But she saw the moment he decided to back away. Saw the decision, and disappointment, in his eyes.

But before he could move, the ship jolted again, throwing her back. And sending him toppling. He caught himself, his arms straining under the momentum. His body was a delicious weight on top of her, though he managed to keep from crushing her. The sudden contact, though, overrode whatever determination he'd had in place. He stared down at her, eyes narrowed, breathing as though he'd run the length of the ship. His arms bent slightly, allowing more of his body to rest against hers, and she gasped, her eyes nearly fluttering closed.

That was all it took. He brushed his lips across hers, and she brought her hand up to his cheek, wanting to hold him captive. His mouth moved against hers in a demanding dance that made her head spin. She threaded her fingers through the hair at the nape of his neck, urging him to deepen the kiss.

The ship heaved again, and Philip wrenched himself from

her, staggering back. He stared down at her, chest heaving, his face unreadable.

"My apologies, my lady. I—" He clenched his jaw. Every muscle in his body looked poised and ready to attack. It must be what he looked like when preparing for battle. Except this time, he wasn't facing an enemy with a sword. He warred with himself. Or perhaps her. She knew exactly how he felt. He drew in a deep breath, his eyes flashing in a face that seemed chiseled from stone. "It willna happen again."

"Philip," she said, pushing herself upright. Could he not tell how much she'd enjoyed his kiss? How much she wanted more?

Or perhaps that was the problem. He knew. And he wanted her just as much.

"I'll leave ye for a moment so ye can change out of those wet clothes before ye catch yer death. I willna be long."

He stepped away from her, slowly, as if he expected her to launch herself at him. And she wanted to. More than he could know. But she had her pride. She wouldn't beg for his touch. When the time came, he'd be the one begging her.

And she'd repeat that to herself until she believed it, because she couldn't help but fear she'd be the one begging.

Chapter Seven

The dock was an overwhelming cacophony of noise and bustling activity that captivated Alice. She hadn't had time to watch the comings and goings when she'd boarded the ship. She'd been far too concerned with getting aboard before Philip arrived. But now, she watched the sailors scurry about the docks like ants on a sweet roll, her imagination running wild at all the things these men must have seen during their travels.

She also kept a close eye on Philip. He'd been far too quiet since their kiss that first night on the ship. The following two days had been full of tense avoidance that had her on edge. Oh, he'd escorted her around the ship as he'd promised. But he'd done so with a brooding silence that drove her to distraction. He seemed to enjoy keeping her in the dark about what would happen once they reached shore, despite her constant inquiry. Or perhaps he merely didn't want to speak to her.

He'd agreed to take her to Elizabet. But he'd done so under duress, to keep her from alerting the authorities. Now that they were in Scotland, that threat didn't hold much weight. Oh, there were still English authorities to whom she could turn. But this was Philip's home. He could disappear without a trace before she could say a word to anyone—and they both knew it.

Not that she'd risk saying anything to anyone. Unless she managed to have him apprehended right there in the street—which would certainly cause her just as much trouble, as she'd be shipped back to her family posthaste—then she couldn't raise the alarm once he'd gone. As his destination was Elizabet and John, sending soldiers after Philip was tantamount to sending them right to Elizabet's doorstep. Something she'd never do. So, there wasn't much she could say now to blackmail him into helping her. She'd simply have to hope he'd honor his agreement.

He'd overseen the unloading of the supplies he'd brought along, as well as her trunk. But while his supplies had been loaded onto a waiting wagon, with him directing the placement of each with the precision of a master clockmaker, her trunk still sat on the road beside it. And for the last several minutes, he'd been conversing with an older gentleman who stood with two women about Alice's age. Philip clapped the man on the shoulder and handed him a small purse. Then he gestured to a couple of boys standing nearby who ran over and picked up Alice's trunk. Except, they didn't stow it on Philip's waiting wagon. They carried it back down the dock toward another waiting ship.

"What's going on?" she said, hurrying over to them. "Where are they taking my trunk?"

"To yer ship," Philip said.

She sputtered, unable to force anything out past the surprise and outrage that flooded through her.

"This is Mr. Forsythe. He's an associate of mine who, great fortune would have it, is returning to England. On that ship," he said, pointing to the ship where her trunk was even now being carted up the gangplank. "And he's agreed to chaperone ye on yer journey back home."

"My what?"

"His two daughters will keep ye company. Ye'll have to share a cabin with them, but I'm sure that'll be no hardship."

"I'm not going anywhere. Bring my trunk back, this instant!"

Mr. Forsythe gave Philip a tight but amused smile and ushered his daughters toward the dock.

"We'll see you aboard, my lady," he said, tipping his hat to her.

Her mouth dropped, and she rounded on Philip. "This was not our agreement."

He completely ignored her, instead taking her arm and turning her in the direction of the ship. "Allow me to escort ye—"

"You'll do no such thing." She yanked her arm from his grasp. "You agreed to take me to Elizabet. And now you'll go back on your word of honor?"

His eyes narrowed. "I've never gone back on my word of honor. However, my word was given to John, first and foremost. His safety and that of his lady supersedes all else. Especially the whims of a spoiled child. Besides, there is no breach of honor, as I never agreed to take ye to Lady Elizabet. I agreed to take ye to Scotland. And here ye are."

"But…you said I could get an audience with the Lion…"

"I said *maybe* ye could. I never said I'd help ye and I certainly never said I'd take ye to them."

She sucked in a breath, momentarily struck dumb by his double-crossing. The desire to eviscerate him where he stood burned through her, but spending the rest of her days in a Scottish prison for murder didn't seem much fun. She'd have to wait until there weren't so many witnesses.

He smirked when she didn't have a retort and turned back to the man loading his cart. Her head spun but she tried to keep her wits about her. She had mere moments to come up with a plan that would not land her back in her family's and her betrothed's clutches.

Watching the man who was supposed to accompany her back home with his daughters, an idea occurred to her. It wasn't the best plan in the world. In fact, she would probably be found out almost immediately. But she refused to stand by while her carefully plotted escape was thwarted. She waited until Philip was busily distracted, overseeing the last trunk being loaded onto his cart and arranging payment for whatever his helpers had done.

"All right, then," she said, rounding on him.

He glanced at her briefly, eyebrows raised, before he turned his attention back to the men who waited on him.

"I shall not force my presence on you any longer. If you refuse to keep your word, then so be it. I'll find another way."

"If ye insist," he said. "As long as ye find it after ye return to yer parents, where ye'll be safe."

She glared at him, gave an exaggerated *humph*, turned on her heel, and marched over to where Mr. Forsythe waited with his daughters. She smiled sweetly at the trio, knowing Philip couldn't see her with her back turned.

Time to once again take matters into her own hands.

. . .

Philip stepped back into the sunshine, letting his eyes adjust to the brightness after the dim interior of the inn. The cart was packed, the barnacle on his back named Alice had been summarily dealt with, and his efforts had been rewarded with a bracing whisky. Time to get back to Glenlyon where he'd be free of the machinations of misbehaving ladies. He refused to dwell on the nagging pit that steadily grew in his stomach at the thought of this particular lady being sent back into the arms of a man she did not want. Who did not deserve her. Even if he wasn't a murderous bag of slime as Alice thought, she still did not wish to wed him. And Philip, despite himself, grew more loathe to send her back.

That kiss aboard the boat had shaken him to his core. More than he wanted to admit. He hadn't been able to avoid her for the rest of their time on the ship, but he'd done his best to keep his distance. Continuing their journey once the ship had made land was something he couldn't allow. She rattled him. Upset his carefully balanced world. And the only way he would restore the order he desperately craved was to eject her from his life as quickly as possible. The fact that doing so was also in her best interest merely solidified his determination to send her back to her family. And the man who waited to wed her.

A man who wasn't him.

He grimaced and tried to bury the memory of her lips moving against his. The feel of her soft body melting against his own.

He shook his head. She wasn't his to moon over. And he didn't want her to be. Sending her home was for the best.

For both of them.

Maybe he needed a few more drinks.

He checked the wagon one last time, tucking in a corner of the canvas covering that was perfectly fine and then turned to find Alice. He wasn't going to rest easy until he saw her physically board the ship. She'd flounced past the inn window with one of Forsythe's daughters a few times, ensuring he saw her anger. He'd seen it, all right. It still brought a smile to his lips.

He shaded his eyes with his hand and scanned the harbor. The ship looked to be moments from departing. He caught sight of Forsythe following his daughters up the gangplank. Several yards ahead of them, the wide-brimmed hat and overly trimmed cape of the annoyingly delectable Lady Alice was stepping onto the deck of the ship and making her way swiftly below. Apparently, she had no wish to wave goodbye to him as the ship departed. Couldn't say he blamed her.

Philip released a pent-up breath. The weight that had been resting on his shoulders from the moment Lady Alice had barged her way into his room at the boardinghouse lifted, along with the anchor on the ship. He tried not to dwell on the pang that hit him at the thought of her sailing out of his life. Now that she was safely on her way back home and soon to be her father's problem once again, Philip could admit to himself that a small part of him was sorry to see her go. A very small part. Tiny. She'd been amusing, at the very least. But the woman was nothing but trouble and far too distracting. They were both better off with her gone.

With that done, he hopped up onto the driver's seat of his wagon and flicked the reins in his hand to get the horses moving. Time to go home. Where the headstrong, spirited women were all safely married to his kinsmen and none of his concern.

He traveled for several hours, wanting to put as much distance between himself and the docks as possible. The roads thus far were still fairly well-traveled, and it was slow going with the heavily laden cart. He'd be much more at ease once he reached the less populated areas of the Highlands. It would be easier to spot enemies coming when there weren't so many faces to watch.

Up in the distance, the warm glow of an inn's lights beckoned him. He'd sleep in the heather for the remaining nights of his journey. But he'd get one night in a good bed before he'd leave the main road. He pulled the wagon into the shed on the side of the inn and beckoned to one of the stable boys.

He held up a dirk. "Ye ken how to use this?"

The boy nodded, his eyes darting from Philip to the weapon.

Philip jerked his head at the wagon. "Keep an eye on that wagon for me until I leave in the morning, and if no harm comes to it, the dirk is yers to keep. Can ye do that?"

"Aye, my lord," the boy said, enthusiastically nodding his head.

"Good lad." Philip took a coin from his sporran and tossed it to him.

He looked over everything one last time and was about to turn around when a slight movement caught his attention. He froze, his hand on his sword. The boy frowned and opened his mouth, but Philip put a finger up to his lips and the boy nodded, though he kept a keen eye on the wagon.

Philip waited, his body tensed to react. His eyes roved over the wagon. There it was again!

This time he lunged, his hand plunging beneath the canvas until he grasped something warm, firm, and very much alive. His prisoner gasped and slapped at his hand. He ignored her, ripping away the canvas so he could haul her out of the wagon.

"What the hell are ye doing here?" he all but growled at Alice who stood trembling and disheveled but as defiant as ever in his iron grasp.

"Making sure you keep your word." She jutted that pert little nose of hers in the air, acting for all the world like she had not just been caught as a stowaway.

"I saw you get on that ship."

Her lips twitched in a defiant half smile that sent his blood thundering through his veins. And not just because he was angry.

"You saw the Misses Forsythe get on that ship. Preceded

by their maid, who was happy to trade her cooperation in my plan for my new hat and cloak. The Misses Forsythe gladly kept their father occupied long enough for her to board the boat in my stead. I believe they had a rather fun time fooling their father. Poor dears are rather bored, never allowed to have any fun."

"They'd do no such thing."

Alice snorted. "Obviously, they did. Women tend to stick together, Mr. MacGregor. At least in some matters. I promise you, they were more than happy to help me. Especially as they'll get to keep my trunk and its contents as payment."

Philip released her and stalked to the end of the shed and back. Twice. He didn't worry she'd bolt the moment he released her. Hell, he apparently couldn't rid himself of the woman even when he tried. Her sheer tenacity would be admirable if it didn't fly in the face of everything he'd so carefully planned.

On his third pass, he stopped in front of her and planted his hands on his hips, thoroughly prepared to give her the dressing down she so richly deserved. She crossed her arms and raised an eyebrow, waiting.

He pointed his finger at her and opened his mouth. Then closed it. Opened it once more. But when that eyebrow quirked up even farther with obvious amusement, he blew out a frustrated breath and threw his hand down.

"Bah!" he said, unable to come up with a single, solitary thing to say that would make a dent in that stubborn, thick head of hers.

He turned on his heel and stalked toward the inn. Like it or not, he was stuck with her. Again.

He entered the inn with her hot on his heels. He would deal with her later. Once he was full of good food and ale. If he was lucky, maybe he could avoid her until morning. A good night's rest wouldn't come amiss, either.

Of course, once she slid onto the bench across from him he realized there would be no escape. A loud grumble from the general direction of her stomach sent a shard of guilt stabbing through him. She'd been hidden in that cart since that morning and likely hadn't eaten the entire day. Albatross around his neck or no, he couldn't let her starve.

He had a quick word with the innkeeper and arranged a room for the evening. Only one, unfortunately, as that was all they had available. Not ideal, to be certain. But he'd deal with the implications of it once they'd eaten. He thought better on a full stomach.

He ordered them both large portions of the inn's stew and a loaf of crusty bread. For a blissful five minutes, they didn't speak while they shoveled spoonfuls of surprisingly tasty food into their mouths. He knew the truce wouldn't last, but he was damn well going to enjoy it while he could.

Which didn't turn out to be long. She finished long before he did and began peppering him with questions.

"How far are we from Glenlyon?"

He took his time finishing the food in his mouth before answering. "Four days journey. Maybe five."

"That far?"

He shrugged and ripped off another piece of bread. "Faster without the wagon. Faster still without you."

She ignored that. "So, we must spend at least three more nights together."

"Aye," he said. "Except tomorrow we'll not have a fine inn in which to lay our heads. Ye'll have to sleep in the rough, with naught but a fire and my goodwill to keep ye safe."

She scowled at him but didn't seem overly concerned. They both knew he'd protect her with his life. No matter what his personal feelings were. Not that even he could identify them half the time. Aggravating as she was, the imminent prospect of sharing a room with her was conjuring thoughts that had no business being in his head.

His foul mood lasted until they were safely ensconced behind closed doors. While they hadn't completely escaped notice, no one seemed too interested in either of them. A blessing to be sure. This far from London, he didn't expect to run into anyone who would recognize the lady, let alone him. But he wouldn't rest easy until they were safe behind Glenlyon's fortified walls.

Alice looked around the room, her eyes widening slightly as they took in the single bed. "And shall we be sharing this bed, my lord?" She gave him an amused smirk.

He frowned. "No. I'll sleep on the floor. You may have the bed."

Her amusement faded. "That won't be very comfortable."

"It seems an odd time for ye to be suddenly concerned for my comfort, considering yer mere presence on this journey is decidedly against my comfort. Besides, I willna be doing it for my comfort or benefit."

She released an irritated sigh that would have made even his sainted grandmother raise her brows. "Must you always be such a martyr to your honor?" She held up her hand to stave off his immediate rebuttal. "I appreciate the concern for my virtue. However, I think I can trust you not to behave in any fashion to which I'd object. The bed is large enough for us both and none would be the wiser."

His mouth quirked up at that. The little minx. Knowing her, there were very few behaviors of his she'd object to. Other than leaving her behind, that is.

"As flattered as I am for yer trust, my lady, I'll be guarding the door against any out there who may have designs on yer virtue. Ye are safe from me, I assure ye."

"I never doubted it," she said, though her frown hinted at disappointment. "Is the protection truly necessary?"

He stared at her. Her supple, smooth skin that blushed

slightly when she was angered...or aroused. Her ringleted hair that still artfully framed her face, despite a day hidden in his cart. The eyes that flashed amber fire with the passion that burned beneath her surface. Oh yes. There would be many a man who would desire a taste of what she had to offer and wouldn't stop to ask if she were willing. But he didn't wish to frighten her. So, all he said was, "Whether they will or no, I'll be there all the same."

"Won't the bolt on the door be protection enough?"

"It should be sufficient, aye. But I'll no' take any chances with yer safety."

Her cheeks flushed at that, and she stared at him, her eyes searing his.

He cleared his throat. "I must check on the wagon before we retire for the night. Bolt the door behind me and open it for none but me. Understand?"

She nodded and came toward him, stopping mere inches away. "And if some unsavory character should try to enter the chamber while you are gone?" She blinked at him, all sweetness and innocence that he knew hid a will of iron.

"Then scream for me, my lady." He gestured to the window behind her. "It overlooks the courtyard. I'll hear ye. But I should hope even you can keep out of trouble for five minutes."

"I shall try," she said, her grin suggesting otherwise.

He shook his head but kept his long-suffering sigh to himself until he'd left her safely bolted in the bedchamber.

If they both made it to Glenlyon alive, it'd be a miracle.

Chapter Eight

Alice watched Philip walk away, admiring the view his kilt-covered backside made as he stalked down the corridor. Once he was out of sight, she ducked her head back in the room and bolted the door, really quite pleased with herself. Though Philip was proving to be a much bigger problem than she'd anticipated. She'd never had to work so hard to get a man to do what she wished. Then again, Philip cared nothing for who her father was, or how large her dowry was, or how close her family was to the king. He did care for her, however, no matter how often he protested the fact. Well, perhaps not on a deeper, personal level...they barely knew each other. But he certainly liked what he saw when he looked at her.

Not that he seemed inclined to do anything about it. The Highland rogue had surprised her at every turn. She hadn't expected him to be so...honorable. She knew any number of supposed court gentlemen who'd have had her on her back with her skirts over her head at the first sign of interest from her. Yet even when she'd almost thrown herself at Philip, he'd held himself aloof. At great personal effort, she could tell, though he'd tried to hide it. But still, he'd managed. So far.

She smiled to herself, thinking of the coming night when the two of them would be closed off together in the small chamber. Any number of things could happen once the candles were extinguished. She fervently hoped his honor disappeared along with the light...and took her virtue with it. Philip was too fine a figure of a man for her not to want him, and their time was running short. She had no idea what her future would bring. But she was bound and determined to control as much of it as possible.

She could admit that she hadn't been so bothered by her life and the conventions that ruled it until they ran contrary to her own wishes. Her life had been wonderful. Full of fine houses, parties, pretty things to wear, amusing friends, and frivolous pastimes. She could even admit that had her parents chosen someone else for her—a dashing young lord or perhaps an ancient but harmless noble who'd leave her a rich widow, without requiring much in return—perhaps she would not have run.

But something about Woolsmere made her skin crawl. A sinister air hung about the man—something in his eyes when he looked at her. She couldn't pinpoint it, couldn't prove anything. But she knew deep down inside that if she wedded him, she'd not be long for the world. And though the match was a prestigious one, it had surprised her how little her parents had taken her feelings into consideration. They'd always been generous and affectionate with her. She didn't doubt they loved her. Yet still, their choice had been made and nothing she'd said had swayed them. And she wouldn't accept that.

She would be in control of her fate. Not her father, or some other man, and certainly not Society's unfair rules. And the giving of her maidenhead was one pleasure she would save for the man *she* chose.

With that thought in mind, she went to the small table in the corner of the room and picked up a pitcher to pour out some wine. Only to find it empty. She sighed and looked around the room. Nothing else suitable to drink. Not even water in the ewer on the stand. A quick glance out the window showed her Philip standing outside the stables giving more instructions to the stable hand. Alice rolled her eyes. Really, handsome though the man may be, his rigid insistence on doing everything a specific, and usually overly complicated way, drove her mad. How difficult was it to tell the child what to do? There's the wagon. Watch it. Don't let anyone touch it. Here's a coin. Simple. She could see the poor child's eyes glazing over even at her distance.

She marched to the door, hesitatingly briefly. He'd told her to stay in the room. For her protection. But her parched throat pleaded otherwise. She'd just open the door and see if there was a chambermaid or someone wandering by she could send to fetch her some wine. The deserted corridor crushed that hope.

The stairs to below were a few scant feet away, and the glow of firelight beckoned warmly to her. She took a deep breath and squared her shoulders. She'd go down, quickly fetch something to drink, and come right back. It was a reputable place. And there were plenty of witnesses below. Philip was being overly cautious.

She marched downstairs, head held high like she had every confidence in the world, as she generally did, even though her current situation was a bit out of the usual for her. Still, she managed to find one of the serving girls, who apologized profusely for the empty pitcher and ewer in the room and promised to bring both wine and water straightaway. Alice made her way toward the room, both proud that she'd taken care of the problem on her own and silly for being at all nervous about disobeying Philip's orders.

She'd nearly gotten to her door when a man stepped from the shadows. She stopped with a gasp that she immediately clamped her mouth shut on. She wouldn't give him the satisfaction of knowing he'd startled her.

"Pardon me," she said, taking a step forward. She expected him to tip his hat and get out of her way.

He did neither.

"What are you doing wandering about the corridors all alone?" he asked. The scent of alcohol on his breath singed her nose.

"I'm not all alone. There are half a dozen people down the stairs, and a maid is following on my heels with some items for my room. As is my husband," she added, when he showed no indication of moving.

"Husband, is it? I doubt any man would leave such a delectable little piece such as you lying about unattended."

That was it. Philip told her to scream if she needed him. Well, she needed him, and she had no qualms about letting everyone in hearing distance know it.

She opened her mouth, but before she could utter a sound, the man's hand clamped around her neck and squeezed.

"None of that now." He pushed her toward her room, his hand squeezing her neck tighter.

She clawed at it, clawed at him. There was no way she was letting him force her into that chamber with him. She prayed Philip would hurry, but for all she knew he was still explaining to the stable boy, in minute detail, the exact way in which one should stare at a wagon all night.

She must get the man's hand off her long enough to scream. That would surely bring someone who could help.

She dug her nails into his forearms and kicked against his shins. Thankfully, she wore the sturdy boots she'd purchased for the trip instead of the delicate slippers she typically wore indoors. Her boots connected with his shin hard enough to make him grunt. His grip loosened enough that she was able to drag in a lungful of air. She let it out with a screech that should have shattered every window in the place.

The man's eyes widened, and he let go. He spun around and came face to face with Philip, who wasted no time in planting his fist in the man's gullet. "Ye dare lay hands on her?" he shouted, following up his swing with one to the chin, which knocked the man to his knees.

"Here now! I didn't know she were your wife. Honest!"

"Wife?" Philip said, the word bringing him up short.

"That's a lie!" Alice said, rage boiling in her until the edges of her vision blurred. "I told you my husband was on his way up, and you assaulted me anyway, you vile, miserable miscreant!" She punctuated each insult with a kick that probably did more damage to the skirts her foot kept tangling in than it did to the man. But it made her feel better.

"No man would let his wife prance around a roomful of drunken men unattended. How was I to know ye werena lying?"

"I was not prancing, you filthy, miserable sot! And lying or not, you have no right to put your hands on me!" She tried to kick at him again, but Philip wrapped his arms around her from behind and lifted her, swinging her away from him.

"Alice, go to the room and wait for me. I'll take care of this," he said, sneering at the man who remained on his knees.

"I'll do no such thing!" she said. She wasn't about to hide away like some frightened little girl. "I want this man arrested. He should be in chains, acting like such an animal."

"Alice," Philip hissed. "We are drawing a crowd."

She opened her mouth to protest that she didn't care, when she remembered that she very much did care. They were supposed to be keeping a low profile and, thanks to her refusal to listen to Philip and a powerful set of lungs, they were now the center of attention of everyone in the inn.

"My lord, I'm so sorry," the innkeeper said, scurrying forward with a couple of large stable hands who promptly hefted the man to his feet. "Dinna mind Mr. Bowman. He doesna think too well when he's in his cups. I hope he's done no damage to yer...wife?"

Alice took in the increasingly curious crowd around them. She stood in the doorway of the chamber she and Philip were obviously sharing. If he refuted that they were wed, her reputation would be irreparable. Though they could surely keep up with the pretense from the ship, that they were siblings...

"Lady Alice? Good heavens, what is going on here?"

Alice closed her eyes and sucked in a deep breath through her nose before she turned to face Mr. Cravens, the proprietor of a confectionary shop she frequented with her mother. So much for the sibling story.

"A simple misunderstanding, Mr. Cravens," she said, coming forward to stand by Philip's side. "I'm afraid this man," she said, nodding at the back of Mr. Bowman, who was being dragged off by the stable hands, "became a little too forward and startled me. My...husband was, of course, merely defending me."

"Your husband? How splendid, I hadn't heard you'd wed."

He gave a polite smile to Philip that didn't quite reach his eyes. To his credit, he gave no indication of the shock he must be feeling to find the daughter of Lord Morley in the middle of such a commotion while her glowering, thoroughly Scottish, supposed husband stood watch over them.

"Yes, we are married. Only just... Isn't that right, husband?"

She turned to him, her eyes pleading. If Philip denied her now...

He gave the man a tight smile. "Aye, we're wed. Only

just." His eyes glanced at the crowd around them, and he seemed to come to some sort of decision. He squared his shoulders and raised his voice, so everyone gathered about could hear him.

"This is my wife," he said, wrapping his arm around Alice's waist and drawing her to him. "I want there to be no misunderstanding in case anyone else here had any misconceptions. As her husband, she is under my protection and I'll defend her with my last breath. Is there anyone else who wishes to challenge me?"

"No, no, of course not," the innkeeper said, trying to shoo everyone away. "I'll have some of my best whisky brought up straightaway, my lord. And I'll make sure Mr. Bowman isna able to trouble anyone else again tonight."

Philip nodded at him and turned on his heel, keeping his hold on Alice until they were safe in their chamber. He closed the door on the rest of the curious faces in the hall and bolted it.

Then he released a long, drawn-out sigh and tiredly rubbed a hand over his face.

"All ye had to do was stay in the chamber another five minutes. And ye couldna even do that."

She had the grace to give him a sheepish smile. "I know it wasn't the most prudent thing to do, but I was so thirsty, and I didn't think it would do any harm to quickly order some wine."

"Aye, ye didna think. Ye never think. Ye follow whatever silly impulse comes into yer head. And now an inn full of people is aware of our presence and kens who ye are. And that ye're now my wife."

Alice blinked at him, not sure she heard that last bit correctly. "You mean, they think I'm your wife. What harm is there in a few strangers being under the misconception that we are wed?"

He loosed another long-suffering sigh. "We declared each other man and wife, with clear intent, in front of assembled witnesses. In Scotland, that is enough to be legally binding. For a time, at least."

Her stomach flipped, and all the blood rushed to her head and back out again with enough force to make her dizzy. She'd joked about wedding him. Dreamed about it a time or two. But surely, merely stating that they were wed in front of an audience wasn't enough...

Though judging by the tortured look on Philip's face, it was.

"Well then..." she said, releasing a long breath of her own. "How shall we spend our wedding night?"

Chapter Nine

Philip looked at her with such an expression of shock, bordering on horror, that Alice almost laughed.

"I think I'd be offended by that look on your face if I didn't realize it was due to surprise and not a total lack of desire. Because we both know that is not true."

He stared at her, but before he could say anything a knock sounded on the door. He turned to answer it and let in serving maids with pitchers of water, wine, a decanter of whisky, and a selection of crusty bread, cheese, meat, and fruit. Someone was trying to keep them happy.

"My father wishes ye a long and happy marriage," one of the girls said.

Philip nearly spit out the whisky he'd sipped.

"That's very kind of him," Alice said, walking the girls out. "Be sure to convey our thanks."

Once she had the door bolted, she turned around to watch her supposed husband. It still didn't seem quite real. Or legal, despite his explanations. She supposed it was similar to handfasting.

Now that it had happened, it didn't seem so crazy. It would solve quite a few of her problems. Even if she were to be found, her parents would not be able to force her to marry the man of their choosing as she was already wed. In a way. She assumed they'd have to have it blessed by the church and sign some paperwork or something in the future to make it truly legal. But for the moment, she was safely Philip's wife.

As long as he didn't get it into his thick skull that she'd suddenly start following his orders. She'd begun this whole adventure to remove herself from anyone's control. Wed or not, she would continue to follow her own counsel when it pertained to her life. No accidental wedding was going to change that. Philip would simply have to reconcile himself to a wife with a mind of her own. She had no doubt she could eventually bend him to her ways. Well, she had some doubts. He'd already proven vastly more stubborn than any other man she'd ever dealt with.

And she supposed her circumstances would be much changed. She still found herself married to a man she barely knew but heading for a life a great deal more mysterious than the one she had left. She could admit to herself that that was part of the appeal. Marriage to the old earl would make her life nothing but an endless chain of soirées and balls. If she were lucky. His other wives had rarely been seen in public after the wedding breakfast. Her only function would have been to obey her husband in everything he said and to be an ornament for him to show off, to do with as he pleased.

The same could probably be said of Philip. But at least he was a rugged, young, virile, and incredibly handsome man who set her blood afire with a mere look. And her body with the slightest touch. She might quite enjoy obeying his orders. At least some of them. Some of the time. The ones she liked, in any case.

Besides, the two women she knew of who had run off

with MacGregor men were both utterly content. Sorcha MacGregor had been married off to the Laird of Glenlyon, the one they called The Lion. From what Alice had heard, Sorcha had been quite against the match, yet from Elizabet's letter, Sorcha had not only come to terms with her marriage but was blissfully happy, living with her warrior in one of the most beautiful places that Elizabet had ever seen.

Elizabet herself had run off with Philip's kinsman John. A highwayman who still had a price on his head. Elizabet had grown up in circumstances much the same as Alice's. Yet she was not suffering for her choices. In fact, according to her letter, Elizabet seemed ecstatically happy.

Neither one of these women had begun their relationships loving or even knowing their men. Yet everything had turned out wonderfully for them. Philip was, of course, a different man. However, if Alice had to choose between him and the old earl, she would much rather take her chances with Philip. At the very least, she would not cringe when he touched her. In fact, she looked forward to it.

"It's really not all that bad, if we are, indeed, married," she said.

Philip put down the cup of whisky he'd drained and looked at her, eyes wide with shock. "Ye canna mean that," he said.

"Yes, I do." She crossed her arms and drew herself up straight, staring directly into his eyes. "If my choices are to marry you or be bundled off to the murderous old codger who thinks he has bought my hand, my life…then I choose you."

Philip's jaw worked open and shut a few times as if he couldn't quite decide how to respond to that. She stepped near enough to place her hand on his arm. He looked down at her with an expression she couldn't identify, but which sent a fine shiver through her that wasn't altogether unpleasant.

"I know this isn't what you might wish. But I don't see that we have any other choice. All those people out there... and Mr. Cravens. It will get back to my family, no matter what we do now."

Philip's eyes opened even wider. "Aye. I ken that very well. But that doesna mean we have no choice in the matter."

She folded her arms across her chest and glared at him. "You'd let me be ruined when such a simple solution—"

"Simple solution?"

"You know what I mean."

He sighed and shook his head again. "It's no' the way things are done."

It took a supreme effort to keep from rolling her eyes. "I know you like to follow the proper order of things, but sometimes circumstances demand unorthodox actions."

He snorted at that. "Every moment with you has been unorthodox."

She gave him half a grin. "Is that so bad?"

"Aye. Ye have no idea."

"Philip..."

He jammed his hand through his hair and stalked away from her for a second, frustration rolling off him in waves. When he paced back to her, she raised a brow, waiting for whatever was boiling beneath his surface to finally erupt.

He closed his eyes and took a deep breath, releasing it slowly. When he spoke again, his voice was calm, slow, and measured, as if he were speaking to a small child. Or a skittish horse.

"Alice. Ye canna be thinking this through clearly."

Was he afraid she was going to kick him in the backside if he spooked her? She hadn't planned on it, but if he kept talking to her in that tone of voice, she might.

"Ye canna wish to wed me. We dinna even ken each other. I'm far below your station—"

"That doesn't matter—" she said, trying to wave that concern away.

"And even if that were no' true," he continued, not letting her finish, "I dinna have any wish to be shackled with a wife."

Alice narrowed her eyes at him and leaned in closer. "And what is our other option? If you denounce me now, Mr. Cravens will run straight to my father. I'll be ruined and so will you, because my father will hunt you down. If Mr. Ramsay isn't already aware that we are here, then the last thing you should want is more attention brought to us."

His eyes narrowed, and she resisted the urge to step back. "I wouldna have any attention on me at all if it wasna for you."

"You don't know that. You said yourself that Ramsay had probably been watching my residence. Which means he very well may have seen you coming and leaving. He might have followed me, but he could have followed you. Regardless, even if he were not aware of you or your whereabouts, being involved in a scandal involving Lord Morley's daughter would make sure he would be shortly apprised. The only way to keep everyone quiet and protect both ourselves and our friends is to present ourselves as married."

"Ye're mad."

She shrugged. "No. Just practical. Besides, what's done is done. We both declared ourselves wed in front of witnesses and according to you, that's all we need. We can deal with it later. You can divorce me, annul the marriage, or live separately from me."

He glowered darkly at her, and she decided to change tactics. She did want this marriage to be…amicable, after all.

"Or," she said, stepping a little closer, "maybe you'll surprise yourself and enjoy the fact that we are married. There are certain advantages, or so I've been told," she said, giving him her best smoldering look.

Either she was losing her touch or Philip was completely immune because the only response she got from that was a raised eyebrow. The intense look that remained in his eyes was more likely due to anger than lust. Pity.

She sighed, stepping away. "Fine. Suit yourself. My one desire is to escape the life I had no hand in choosing and find my friend who is the one person in this world I can trust to understand. I simply ask that you stay married to me for the time being. Do what you will with me once we arrive at Glenlyon. I do not care."

"Oh, ye'll care, my lady," Philip said, closing the distance she'd put between them, his eyes flashing with a sudden heat. "As my wife, ye're mine. To do with as I please. Is that what ye wish?"

Alice's mouth went dry. Perhaps he wasn't as immune to her as he wanted to appear. She swallowed hard. "If you are trying to scare me, it will not work." She let her gaze roam over him, trying to show him exactly how willing she was to call his bluff. "I've already made it clear I am more than happy to be your wife. In every way." Then she shrugged. "But willing or no, I don't see that we have any other choice. Publicly, at least."

Philip stared down at her for long enough that she didn't think he'd answer. Those stark blue eyes of his bored into hers, his entire body seething with confusion and anger… and a vitality that she had never experienced in any of the dandified men with whom she'd dallied at court. Oh yes, if she had to be wed to a man she did not love, the one before her would do very nicely.

Finally, Philip drew in a great breath, gave her a last exasperated look, and then turned back to the table holding the whisky and refreshments. "I need a drink."

• • •

Philip stood stock-still, staring out the window. His mind was too overwhelmed with the recent events to do more than watch the retreating back of Mr. Cravens. Philip had hoped to have more time to reach Glenlyon, but they'd have to make all haste now. He didn't know how well Mr. Cravens knew Alice's family. But it wouldn't take much to have them on their tail.

He took another long sip of whisky, savoring the way the amber liquid slid down his throat, while his mind whirled. One minute, he'd been boarding the boat, breathing a sigh of relief to be journeying back to Scottish soil. The next, he'd been saddled with a runaway wife who was leaning against the wall of his chamber looking as if she were daring him to kiss her again. And that was something he absolutely could not allow to happen. No matter how badly he wanted to comply.

And oh, he wanted to. He hadn't planned to kiss her that night at the ball. Or on the ship. But when that soft, full mouth had pressed against his, his body had taken over. She'd met every move of his lips, every thrust of his tongue, with a heated enthusiasm that bordered on desperation. And he'd been right there with her. Desperate. Hungry. Aching for more. It had taken every ounce of willpower to pull away from her.

He'd known the little vixen had fire in her blood. He'd never met a woman so badly in need of a tumble in all his days. It just hadn't occurred to him that one touch of her lips and he'd be hard pressed to keep from doing the tumbling himself. But if he ever wanted to be rid of her, he was going to have to keep his hands off.

Which was going to be much easier said than done now that he'd publicly claimed her as his wife.

Her gaze raked over him, and he had to clench his fists to keep from reaching for her. She gave him a slow, sensuous smile. "Now that I'm your wife, I suppose there is no need for you to spend the night on the floor."

His lips twitched. "More need now than there was before, I'd say."

Her full lips pushed into a pout. "I don't see how that is true." She stepped closer. "Will you at least kiss your wife, my lord?"

He shook his head. "There willna be another kiss. The first was a mistake."

"A mistake?" She raised a delicately shaped brow. "Then what about the second?"

"Aye, that was a mistake, too."

"And the third?"

"There willna be a third."

Her eyes narrowed slightly at the gruff tone of his voice, and he was sorry if he offended her. But one of them had to keep their wits about them. For her sake.

"I know I'm not the only one who feels something between us," she said, moving close enough she could run her hands up his chest.

He grasped them, squeezing them tightly to take away the sting of rejection before he pushed her away. He didn't want to hurt the lady. But he had no intention of doing anything else with her, either. Best she understood that.

"Someday, lass, in the very near future, when ye're tired of rough living and wish to return to yer palaces filled with silks, and jewels, and all the creature comforts ye'll no' find with me, ye'll thank me for having the presence of mind to keep ye intact."

She scoffed. "The only thing any man at court will care about is that my fortune is intact and there's no babe brewing in my belly that I might try to foist off on them. As long as we are careful, we can avoid that. Truthfully, a few of the older, more incapable gentlemen desperate for an heir would not even mind the babe. So your gallantry, while appreciated, isn't needed. Or wanted. There is something else I desire."

She drew a finger down his chest, and he had to grit his teeth to keep from leaning in to her touch.

He stopped her hand when it reached his waist. "I have no interest in what ye have to offer."

Her eyes glanced downward. "The arrangement of your pleats say otherwise."

Philip scowled, well aware that his kilt did little to hide his arousal. "Ye should be thankful that I'm no slave to my urges."

"*Hmm*, I find it a pity more like. And a surprise, to be honest. I didn't expect a rough Highland laird to be so... virtuous."

He snorted. "Too much like your suitors at court for your liking?"

She laughed. "On the contrary. Most of the courtiers of my acquaintance would have had my skirts around my ears at the first invitation. As long as we were discreet about it."

"And did ye also expect me to woo ye with songs and posies? Because I'm afraid I'll have to disappoint ye on that as well."

She waved him away. "I spent my formative years on the Continent and have been in Charles's court since he returned. I've been surrounded by his Cavaliers for years. Those overly devoted Royalist remnants from his father's court, whose ranks have swelled with their new Cavalier King's return. With their exhausting and all-consuming love of wine, women, and king, frankly, I've been romanced to death. I'm done with romance. And foppish men who are more interested in peacockish posturing bedecked in couture and cosmetics than actually pleasing a woman. What I want is a big strong man who flatters no one yet knows what to do with his hands."

He knew what to do with his hands, all right. Keep them to himself. No matter how much he wanted to rip open her bodice and fling her skirts aside. "Again, my lady. I'm sorry to disappoint ye."

She sighed deeply. "You are taking this far too seriously."

He raised an eyebrow at that. "Marriage? Ye think I'm taking holy matrimony too seriously?"

"There's nothing holy about our matrimony until it's blessed in the eyes of the church. Which neither of us has any desire to do. Regardless, yes. You're taking it far too seriously."

He laughed at that. A great, rolling belly laugh that he hadn't experienced in more time than he could remember.

Her eyes narrowed but shone with amusement. "Laugh all you want. I'll seduce you yet, husband."

He grinned at her. "Ye're welcome to try, wife. But I'll think ye'll find my virtue not so easily won."

"*Hmm.* We shall see." She gave him a smile that hit him right in his core. "The sun has set. Perhaps you'll be more inclined to perform your husbandly duties on our wedding night by the light of the moon."

He snorted. "There will be no wedding night."

"That's not strictly true. After all, we were wed, after a fashion, and darkness has fallen. Hence, a wedding night." She stared up at him through her lashes, looking for all the world like an innocent angel.

He narrowed his eyes at her. "If you wish to call it so."

"I do." She sauntered over to the bed and sat down, leaning back on her hands. A position which put her tightly encased bosom on delightful display. "So, what shall we do to wile away the hours? I'm not a bit sleepy."

At the moment, a refreshing dip in the freezing ocean sounded like a fine idea. Not very practical, though, as they were miles from the shore.

His new bride was going to be a handful.

"Sleepy, or no, ye'll rest for a few hours. We'll leave before the sun rises."

She frowned at that, all trace of teasing gone from her face. "Why so early?"

"Because yer Mr. Cravens has seen fit to depart the inn in the dark of night, which seems a verra peculiar thing to do. At best, some urgent business called him away. More likely, he is off to make yer whereabouts known to yer family. And what yer family kens, Ramsay will soon find out. It'd be best if our whereabouts changed before that occurs. We need to reach Glenlyon before our enemies."

Sometime in the night, Philip was woken by the sound of thrashing on the bed. A muted keening had him jumping up from the cold floor. Alice lay tangled in the sheets. The heartbreaking sound broke from her lips again, and her face puckered as if in pain.

"My lady," he said, sitting carefully beside her.

She didn't wake. He touched her shoulder and she thrashed again, her breath coming in heaving gulps.

"My lady," he tried again, trying to restrain her movements. It seemed to make her terror worse. "My lady. Alice."

She calmed slightly at the sound of her name. He climbed in beside her and gathered her in his arms, unable to stand the sight of her torment any longer. "Alice. *Shhh.* I've got ye, lass. Rest easy. *Shhh.*"

He cradled her, softly rocking her until she stilled. A sudden stiffness in her limbs alerted him to her wakefulness. But she didn't pull away. If anything, she snuggled closer.

"Are ye all right, my lady?" he asked.

She nodded, but kept her head pressed again his chest. The damp warmth of tears soaked through his shirt. He held her closer.

"What is it?" he asked, softly stroking her back.

"It was my fault. They were dead. Elizabet, John, all of them. And it was all my fault," she said, sobbing against him.

His stomach twisted at the despair in her voice. "Dinna fash," he said, holding her closer still and rocking her gently. "It was naught but a dream."

She burrowed in closer, and he kissed the top of her head, whispering to her until she calmed. He held her until she drifted back into an uneasy sleep, praying that he was right. If Ramsay were to find their friends, it wouldn't matter whose fault it was. The devastation would happen all the same. But he feared she'd blame herself for the rest of her days. As he'd be blaming his own failures. God willing, they'd all remain safe from Ramsay's enraged vendetta.

When he tried to release her to return to his post on the floor, she stirred, her forehead crinkling into a frown even in her sleep. He knew he should extract himself from her arms. But he couldn't bring himself to leave her. And so, he lay beside her, wrapping his body around hers.

He might not be able to keep her safe in the future, though he'd give his life trying. But for one night, he could hold her close and keep her demons at bay. And maybe his own, as well.

Chapter Ten

Some of the tension Philip had been carrying with him eased when the castle came into sight. Home. Still standing strong on the banks of the loch. People went about their daily chores in the small village spread out around it. The sight filled him with a warm comfort that eased the weight on his shoulders.

The last several days as they'd traveled through the countryside had been strained. Philip had assumed Alice would try to take advantage of the fact that they'd woken up in bed together that night at the inn. Instead, she'd seemed... bewildered. She'd kept more to herself as they'd traveled, at least for the first couple days. Something he'd expected he'd appreciate.

Instead, he found himself sticking close to her side, especially at night. For safety and warmth, it was practical to sleep close. However, they invariably found themselves tangled up together in the morning. A circumstance that merely served to increase the building tension and confusion between them. Especially as with each morning that she woke in his arms, Alice seemed more and more happy to be there. And determined to make him admit he enjoyed it, too.

So it was with great relief that they rode into the courtyard of Glenlyon. One of the stable lads ran to take their horses. Philip helped Alice dismount and turned the reins over with a nod of thanks.

"Where's the laird, Hamish?" he asked him.

"In the library, sir, with milady."

Philip ruffled the lad's hair and sent him on his way. Then he jerked his head at Alice and marched into the castle. To her credit, she marched right along with him. Her eyes took in everything—the tapestry-lined halls, the castle folk bustling to and fro, signs of health and prosperity everywhere.

Pride swelled within him. The castle hadn't always been so. Before the Lady Sorcha had married his laird and kinsman Malcolm MacGregor, the castle had been falling down around their ears. Not for lack of love, but the MacGregors had spent so much time locked in a centuries-old feud with Sorcha's clan, the Campbells, that they had not time or money to spend on their home. Everything had been put into the skirmishes against their rival.

Once the king had forced Malcolm, or The Lion as his people liked to call him, to marry Sorcha, the daughter of the Campbells' chief, the war between the clans had stopped, though the animosity would always be there. And there were remnants of their feud. Ramsay, for one. The son of the old Campbell chief, Ramsay had decided to take matters into his own hands and had attempted to both overthrow his father when the laird had called a truce and defeat the MacGregors. It had not ended well for him. He'd been sent to England with his tail between his legs where he'd set himself up as a smuggler. And again, a MacGregor had been his downfall.

John MacGregor had gone and fallen in love with Lady Elizabet, the daughter of Ramsay's partner in crime, Lord Dawsey. While Lord Dawsey and Ramsay had managed to get John arrested for being a highwayman, his punishment hadn't been what they'd hoped. As the king was a friend, John had managed to escape with a sentence of exile. Dawsey was in disgrace, and Ramsay's smuggling enterprise had been dismantled. Nowhere near good enough a punishment for either of them in Philip's mind. But naturally, too dear a price in theirs.

And Ramsay would love to exact retribution for his change in circumstance. Exiled, John shouldn't be back in Scotland. But as long as he stayed out of England and kept a low profile, the king would be happy to look the other way. However, were Ramsay to discover John's whereabouts, the king would be forced to take action against the former highwayman.

Not that Philip thought it would get that far. Ramsay wasn't the type of man to wait on the king's pleasure. He hated the MacGregors with a passion that would give the Devil himself pause. The MacGregors were a fearsome clan—strong, skilled, and brave. They did not fear Ramsay or the fight that would come were he to attack Glenlyon again. But the casualties on both sides would be great, and Philip, for one, would rather avoid unnecessary bloodshed.

Something that would be impossible if Alice's rash actions were to bring Ramsay back to their doorstep.

He watched her as she looked around the keep and was surprised at the hint of anxiety he felt as he waited for her reaction. He wanted her to like his home.

She smiled at him, and more of the tension that he'd been carrying eased.

Though, her opinion shouldn't matter to him. She shouldn't be here. Her presence was a danger to them all, and her methods of persuasion were nothing short of criminal. She was a thorn in his side, not a damsel to be won over.

He frowned and turned his back on her, striding toward

the library. He didn't wait to see if she followed or not. He knew she would.

He nodded at those he passed but kept his pace brisk and determined. None stopped him, though many stared in open curiosity at the lady trailing him. He took the stairs two at a time and stopped only when he'd reached the library door. As it was slightly ajar, he pushed it open and entered with a brief knock to announce his presence.

Malcolm sat behind a desk set near one of the large windows. One of the changes Lady Sorcha had made to the keep was to enlarge the windows in this room. Philip had never approved. Larger windows were nothing but easier targets, in his mind. But the additional light that now streamed into the room made reading a much easier task.

Malcolm gave him a brief glance, then looked again, eyes round, as he registered Philip's presence. He set down the papers he'd been reading and stood, spreading his arms wide in welcome.

The slight gasp behind him made Philip grin. Malcolm was an imposing figure. They didn't call him The Lion for nothing. His halo of red hair would spread around his head like a mane if he didn't keep it tied back, and he stood head and shoulders above most men. His build betrayed years of hard work and fighting. He could swing a broadsword as though it were made of nothing more than wood. Philip would never want those amber eyes glaring at him in disapproval.

Which was why when he greeted his kinsman, it was with a healthy dose of trepidation considering the extra baggage he'd brought to their doorstep.

"Welcome home, Philip," Malcolm said. "Ye've been gone so long we'd begun to think ye'd deserted us."

Philip grinned. "Never, Cousin."

He turned to his cousin's wife, who hurried toward him from the opposite side of the room where she'd been reading by the fire.

"Philip," she said, wrapping him in a warm hug. "It's so good to see that face of yours again."

He kissed her cheek, truly happy to see her. Her English accent was now tinged with a slight Scottish brogue that brought a smile to his lips. Sorcha, a fiery beauty with raven black hair and piercing blue eyes that he thought could see through a man's soul, looked more like his blood kinswoman than her husband, and Philip felt a deep and genuine affection for her. She may not be family born, but she had the heart of a MacGregor.

"And who is this?" she asked, leaning around him to look at Alice.

Alice gave her a beaming smile. "Lady Alice Chivers," she said, with a slight head bob. "Or, MacGregor, I suppose is more appropriate now that we are wed."

Sorcha and Malcolm looked at Philip, their jaws on the floor. He opened his mouth to speak, then shook his head and marched straight for the whisky decanter. He took a healthy slug right from the bottle, and Malcolm nodded. "Aye. I know the feeling, laddie."

Sorcha glanced at him, one eyebrow raised.

Malcolm snorted. "Dinna look at me like that. Ye ken very well that ye drive me to drink on a regular basis."

"I'm fairly certain you'd be driven to drink regularly even without my influence."

Malcolm grinned and grabbed his wife around the waist, hauling her to him for a sound kiss. "Aye. But 'tis more fun to place the blame on you."

She swatted at him and pushed away, though she exuded happiness with her blushing cheeks and wide smile.

Alice pointed at the decanter Philip held in a death grip. "May I?"

Sorcha's face fell. "Of course! You must be exhausted

and starving as well. And here we stand, yammering away."

She shooed Philip away from the whisky and poured Alice a glass herself, then rang for a servant to bring up some refreshments. In short order, Sorcha had everyone seated comfortably, with a drink and a bite to eat in their hands.

Malcolm drained the last drop from his cup and sat back to study his cousin. "Well, how did all this come about?" he asked, nodding between the two of them.

Alice looked at Philip, her lips slightly turned upward, her eyes shining with amusement as if she were daring him to tell the truth. But she didn't know Malcolm. No one lied to The Lion.

Philip sat forward and straightened his shoulders, hating the words that were about to come from his mouth. He took a deep breath. "Lady Alice wished to visit the Lady Elizabet and asked me to take her."

Malcolm's eyebrow rose. "And ye agreed?"

The rest of Philip's breath rushed out with exasperation. "Of course not. The wee she-devil blackmailed me."

Both Sorcha's and Malcolm's eyes widened at that and glanced at Alice, who merely shrugged with a proud smile. Sorcha bit her lip to hold back her own grin and Philip pushed on, determined to get the whole story out.

"Once the ship docked, I arranged straightaway for her to be returned to her family, as her threats of blackmail were much diminished once we reached Scotland. And I never promised to take her farther than Scotland's shore in any case. But she…tricked me—"

"You tricked me first."

He ignored that and continued as if she hadn't spoken. "And hid in the wagon. I didna discover her until later that night when we arrived at the inn."

Malcolm sat back. "I see," he said, rubbing his finger over his twitching lips. Philip scowled at him.

"So," Malcolm continued. "When were ye wed then?"

"Almost a week ago," Alice said with a smile, cutting in before Philip could say a word. "Did you know that by proclaiming you are wed before witnesses, a couple is considered legally married?" She glanced back and forth between Malcolm and Sorcha but continued on before they could answer. "That would have been a good piece of information to know beforehand, I must say. Though, truth to tell, I'm delighted with the situation."

Philip bit back a groan, though his scowl deepened at the growing amusement on his cousin's face.

"Also," Alice said, "while it is obvious Philip is put out by my slight deception with the whole wagon incident, I'd like to point out that such deception was necessary because the blackguard went back on his word of honor and refused to bring me to Elizabet."

Philip sat forward at that. "Blackguard, is it? And ye question my honor? Ye canna hold a man to a promise he makes under blackmail, ye wee harpy. And besides, I didna promise to bring ye to Lady Elizabet. I agreed to bring ye to Scotland. Which I did. There is no dishonor when I kept my word."

Alice's mouth dropped open. "You tricked me."

"Aye, well ye tricked me as well, so I suppose we're even."

Before either of them could continue with the fight that was brewing, Malcolm held up his hand to silence them. Then he shook his head and turned to his wife.

"Thievin', poisonin', kidnappin', blackmail… Honestly, do women no' ken any other way to get a husband? There are simpler methods."

Alice snorted. "Not when you're dealing with a damn stubborn Scot."

"She's got you there," Sorcha said. When Malcolm raised a brow, she shook her finger at him. "Dinna look at me like that," she said, mimicking him. "Scots on their own are bad enough. But you add MacGregor to their name and you'd dig your heels in if God himself told you to do something you didn't think of first."

Alice nodded. "My thoughts exactly." Her eyes flicked to Philip and then away again, and he frowned at her slightly guilty look.

"I'll admit, I had no intention of making our arrangement…permanent," she said. "I truly had no idea of the custom here. But," she said, before Philip could cut in, "as I've told Philip repeatedly, I have no regrets. In fact, I find my situation vastly improved."

Philip shook his head. "A foolish sentiment, as I've told *ye* repeatedly."

Alice shrugged. "We'll have to agree to disagree."

"Not when it means remaining married," he said.

She shrugged again, and Philip turned to Malcolm in exasperation.

"Surely, in such a situation, the custom will not stand. We meant only a pretense to protect her honor. When it comes to such irregular marriages, there must be genuine intent to be accepted as a wedded couple, or so I've always understood. So surely…"

Malcolm frowned. "As long as there are no legal impediments, all it requires is that there is consent on both sides. That ye stood together before witnesses and declared yerselves wed…well…"

"If there were no witnesses," Sorcha said helpfully, "or at least none who mattered. Who knew you. Then…"

Malcolm nodded. "Aye. As the lady," he said, nodding to Alice, "is English and possibly returning home…" He ignored Alice's grunt of disagreement. "The presence of witnesses wouldna matter so much should the two of ye wish to pretend this never occurred."

Philip's face radiated a triumph that was quickly dashed at Malcolm's next words.

"However. Yer declaration was witnessed by someone who knew the lass, aye?" Malcolm asked, glancing at Alice.

She nodded, and Philip reluctantly nodded as well. Malcolm spread his hands wide and sat back in his chair.

"Such a witness, one who presumably is on his way to inform her family of her new status, changes matters. It's no' merely a few Scottish villagers who believe ye to be wed now. Truthfully, her reputation in the eyes of her own society might be irreparably damaged no matter what. It's rare enough here, and the English certainly dinna approve of such marriages. But at least if she is following the customs of her husband in his own country..." Malcolm shrugged.

"Then our best choice is to remain wed according to your customs or I'm ruined. In both our societies," Alice finished for him.

Malcolm nodded, and Philip clenched his jaw, trying to school his face to betray none of the emotion roiling beneath the surface.

He'd known, of course, what Malcolm would say before he'd said it. Had that blasted Mr. Cravens not been witness to their declaration, they might have had cause to dissolve their informal union. But informal though it was, in Scotland, it was legally binding. And with Alice's family soon to know of it, they were stuck with each other.

Sorcha finally took pity on them. "Well. All the particulars aside, you've had a long journey." She turned to Alice. "I know you're anxious to see your friend, but I'm sure you could do with a nice rest. Or at least a wash and a good meal."

Alice nodded gratefully, and Sorcha stood and held out her hand. "I'll show you to a chamber where you can rest and refresh yourself."

Philip stood as well, and Alice stopped, watching him with a slight frown. "How do I know you won't leave me behind the moment I leave this room?"

Philip rubbed both hands across his face and dragged them through his hair. "By all the saints in heaven, woman, ye've managed to stick to me like a barnacle since we left London. We're a mere thirty-minute ride from Kirkenroch. And apparently, I'm now legally obliged to listen to yer harping."

He tried to keep his tone gruff and disapproving, but he couldn't help the small smile that snuck out before he bit it off. He cleared his throat. "It would do little good for me to leave ye now."

Alice regarded him a few seconds more and then nodded her head. "All right, then. But I swear on all that is holy, Philip MacGregor, if you try to trick me again…"

He snorted. "Ye're the one with all the tricks up her sleeves, remember?"

Her face softened and warmed with pleasure at that. "That I am. A good thing for you to remember, I think."

"I'll no' likely forget," he said, his words coming out much softer than he meant them to.

His gaze remained on her until she was out of his sight. But not his mind. The woman had ingrained herself into his life, and he feared if he stayed with her too much longer, she'd be in his heart and soul as well. He seemed to have no defenses when it came to her. She was wearing him down through sheer persistence. Heaven help him if she truly desired for their union to be a permanent one. Because he was beginning to think she just might talk him into it.

Chapter Eleven

Alice paced across her room yet again, stared at the door, and then started a return trek when it didn't open. Sorcha had escorted her to a richly appointed chamber and had hot water sent up so she could wash. Alice had gratefully taken a moment to refresh herself, but, even with exhaustion seeping through her bones, she had no intention of sleeping. She was so close to Elizabet. So close! If Philip didn't fetch her in the next few minutes, Alice had every intention of escaping and hiking to Elizabet on foot if necessary.

She'd given up waiting and had her hand on the door handle when Philip finally entered. He brushed right past without seeing her and then turned, his brow furrowed until he caught sight of her. His gaze didn't linger. Once he'd assured himself she was still there, he marched the rest of the way in and went straight to the ewer of water on the bureau.

Alice stood, hands on hips, while he washed his face and hands. He glanced at her in the mirror as he dabbed his face dry.

She almost spoke but paused a moment, struck at how

domestic the whole scene was. She'd barely begun to get used to sharing a space with him while on board the ship before it had docked. And aside from the one night at the inn, she'd never shared a room with anyone, let alone a man, before. That this could be her life now, someone always there, sharing her meals, her rooms, her bed… It was an odd prospect. One that filled her with both trepidation and excitement.

Watching Philip wash away the dust from the road was somehow more intimate and personal than collapsing in bed at the end of a long day of journeying had been.

His gaze still held hers in the mirror, and she pushed her sentimental thoughts aside. There were more important things to dwell on at the moment.

"Well?" she asked.

He released a long sigh, dabbing his face once more before dropping the towel and moving toward the fireplace. "Will ye no' let a man wash and rest his weary bones a few minutes? I've been on the road with a wicked-tongued harpy for a week now. Ye wouldna believe how taxing it was." He sank into a chair with a groan.

Her jaw dropped. "Is that so?"

"Oh, aye." He tilted his head back on the chair and closed his eyes. "Nothing but incessant chattering, constant nagging and complaining, and snoring so loud at night I couldna get any rest at all. I could sleep straight through till tomorrow."

She straightened her back, marched over to his chair, and deftly kicked the leg out from under it.

He'd apparently been prepared for that and jumped up before the chair hit the floor. He bent to retrieve it, chuckling under his breath. Then he resettled himself with a sigh and closed his eyes again.

"Ye'll have to be less predictable than that, lass."

"I'll keep that in mind," she said, crossing her arms while she watched him.

He squirmed a bit, trying to get more comfortable. "If ye truly wanted to be my wife, as ye keep insisting, ye could make yerself useful and perform a wifely duty or two."

Her heart near jumped out of her chest. "Oh? And what did you have in mind? Husband."

A jumble of thoughts raced through her head. Had his visit with his kinsman finally knocked some sense into his head? Had he actually accepted their marriage?

Her eyes flicked to the soft bed a few feet away, and she wiped her suddenly damp palms on her gown, not releasing her pent-up breath until her lungs began to burn.

Philip didn't make a move toward her. He didn't even open his eyes. Instead, he lifted one of his legs.

She frowned and planted her hands on her hips. When she made no move to touch him, he cracked open an eye and wiggled his foot.

"Some help removing my boots wouldna come amiss, aye?"

The tension drained from her muscles, and she gave him the unladylike snort that he deserved. He dropped his foot with another chuckle.

Being at home, even for as brief a time as they'd been there, seemed to have lifted some weight from his shoulders. She wasn't entirely sure what to do with this new, somewhat playful side of him. A small but warm spot of hope burned in her that she might have the chance to find out.

She relaxed even more as she watched him, a soft glow of warmth spreading through her. She could get used to such a sight every day. Something about the man before her made her feel...safe. Cared for, even, despite his constant jests to the contrary. She could imagine a certain fondness for him developing over time, a possibility she hadn't wanted to entertain before. Until a slight snore emanated from his general direction.

"Of all the…" She snatched her shoe from her foot and threw it at him, hitting him squarely in the chest.

"Wha—?" He jerked up and looked around, his body ready to spring to action. Until he saw her standing there with her hands on her hips.

He slumped back into his chair with a groan. "Leave me be, woman."

She sucked in a deep breath again, ready to do battle. And then she let it out again with a smile. "Certainly."

She grabbed her cloak from where someone had placed it in the armoire and marched to the door.

"Where are you going?" he asked.

"To see Elizabet. Enjoy your nap!" she called over her shoulder.

She had the door halfway open before he slammed his palm against it, closing it again.

"Ye canna do whatever it is ye take it into yer head to do."

"And why not?" she asked. "What possible reason could you have for delaying going to Elizabet now?"

"Other than being so bone tired I could sleep until St. Michaelmas Day, none. But that willna always be the case. John and his lady are still exiled. Should their presence here be betrayed, they would be in danger. It's worth a fair bit of caution, aye?"

Some of the fight went out of Alice, but she stood her ground. "Agreed. However, there is no danger right at this moment. They aren't that far away, and if you'd simply allow me to go, then you could leave me there and be rid of me for good."

"Oh, aye? Simple as that, is it?"

"I don't see why not. You've made it clear you'd prefer to have nothing to do with me. The only reason I blackmailed you in the first place was so you'd take me to Elizabet. So, you'll forgive me if I'm a bit confused as to why you aren't more eager to deliver me to her and be quit of me. I wouldn't make any more demands of you. You could walk away and that would be that."

"Not likely," he said, though the words were muttered so quietly she almost didn't hear them. He studied her face, his eyes roaming over every angle, every feature. "Do ye *want* me to deposit you at Kirkenroch and walk away forever? Truly?"

He hadn't taken his hand from the door, and he leaned in slightly, his fingers playing with one of her curls. Her mouth went dry at the sudden heat in his eyes as he gazed at her, and she licked her lips to moisten them.

"I wasn't speaking of what I wanted, but what I assumed you would want."

"*Hmm*," he murmured. His eyes searched her for a moment longer, long enough that she thought he might lean in to kiss her again. She tried to keep her breathing even and parted her lips, waiting…ready…

He pushed away from the door and stalked back to his chair. "Malcolm asked that we wait an hour before leaving for Kirkenroch. He sent out a few riders to ensure we werena followed."

"Why didn't you tell me that in the first place?"

His answer was a mischievous grin that had her biting her cheek to keep from smiling in return. "Isn't that a bit overly precautious? We were so careful the whole journey."

"Aye, we were. But it doesna hurt to be overly precautious in some circumstances. Better than obeying every impulse that comes into our heads with no thought of the consequences."

It was a rebuke, and one she deserved, but he said it gently with a small smile so, while she narrowed her eyes at him, she let the remark go. This time.

"Once we are certain all is well, then I'll take ye over. Ye have my word."

She released a long sigh. "Very well." She went to the

chair opposite his and sat down. Well, if she was going to have to wait, she might as well get to know her new husband. And if her incessant chattering, as he so sweetly put it, sped things along a little, so much the better.

"So, tell me about your childhood."

He slapped a hand over his face and groaned. She sat back with a grin.

• • •

"Is that it?" Alice asked, nearly bouncing out of her seat next to him in the wagon.

"Aye, now sit back before ye spook the horses." He couldn't help but smile at the joy in her voice. And on her face. She nearly beamed with it. Her beauty struck him anew. The woman was beautiful even covered in the dust of the road with a sour expression darkening her face. But with her full lips smiling, happiness emanating from her eyes, and excitement fairly radiating off her, she took his breath away.

He turned his attention back to the narrow road that led to the ruined manor house of Kirkenroch. He was pleased to see some restoration was in progress. Malcolm had told him that John and Elizabet were restoring the main living quarters of the house. The rest of the repairs would follow later, but it looked like quite a bit of work had already been done. It warmed his heart to see his kinsman's old home being returned to its former beauty. It had been damaged in the many skirmishes with the Campbell clan over the years. It was good to see such a painful past put behind them.

As they pulled near to the main courtyard, he caught sight of John and Elizabet, shading their eyes to see who approached. He knew the exact second Elizabet recognized Alice, because her joy matched the woman beside him. Despite his determination to remain aloof from Alice and her nonsense and his disapproval of her being here in the first place, he couldn't help the warm glow that spread through him at his role in bringing to pass such happiness, even if he didn't truly understand or approve of it.

The horses trotted to a stop at the gates, and Elizabet was at Alice's side before she had a chance to dismount, slinging questions at her so quickly Alice laughed. She slid down and into Elizabet's arms.

"What is this?" Alice exclaimed, releasing Elizabet long enough to touch her blossoming belly.

Elizabet laughed. "John's son, according to him. I say it'll be a girl."

Philip glanced at his cousin as he jumped down from the cart. "Congratulations, Cousin," he said, grasping John by the shoulders and bestowing a kiss on each of his cheeks.

John laughed and clapped him on the shoulder.

Alice gathered Elizabet in another crushing hug, laughing and cupping her face while laughing some more. They stopped exclaiming over each other long enough to glance over at Philip and John, who were, he was sure, staring at them with twin looks of bemusement.

"Not that we are'na glad to see ye both," John said, nodding at them, "but what are ye doing here? Together?"

Alice jutted her chin in the air, and Philip snorted. "Better break out the whisky. 'Tis a long tale."

John set a few men to unloading the cart while Elizabet ushered them inside and got them settled into some chairs around the hearth in the great hall.

"I'm afraid we have only the one guest chamber," Elizabet said, her brow pulled into a worried frown. "We are still repairing much of the house."

Philip was about to tell her it was no matter, that he'd be comfortable enough in the stables or on a pallet by the hearth, but before he could, Alice cut in.

"Oh, it's no bother. One chamber will be fine. We're married," Alice said, grinning as if it were the happiest news in the world.

Philip snorted at the stunned looks on their hosts' faces. "Ye really need to stop leading off with that," he said to Alice.

She shrugged. "It's the biggest and most relevant news. Why not mention it first?"

"Because unbelievable and upsetting news should be eased into, no' just blurted out. Besides, I dinna see how it's the most relevant news—"

Her mouth dropped open, and she leaned in closer. "Unbelievable and upsetting? How so? Am I so unappealing that marrying me is unthinkable?"

Actually, quite the opposite. It was her wanting to marry *him* that people wouldn't believe. But she didn't pause long enough for him to say that, not that he would have.

"And upsetting? Who has our marriage upset?"

"I believe I've made it perfectly clear that *I'm* upset."

"Oh," she said, waving that off with a little snort. "It's a minor wrinkle in our plan, I'll give you that. But upsetting is going a little far."

"It's no' going nearly far enough! Ye were a right bit criminal in getting me to bring ye all the way here and then I ended up married for my trouble? Fine way to thank a man."

"Well, it's not like I planned for any of this."

"For someone who didna plan much, ye certainly seem to be getting yer way about everything."

"Not everything," she said, pitching her voice lower and looking at him with enough suggestion in her eyes he damn near blushed.

"And how is it *not* the most relevant news?" she added. "Seems to be the biggest piece of news we brought with us."

"Certainly the most interesting, at least," Elizabet piped in, although neither of them was really paying attention to her.

"I dinna ken," Philip said. "Perhaps the fact that ye had to blackmail yer way into this mess is a better, more *relevant*, place to start," he said.

"Oh, *that's* definitely the most interesting part, so far," John said, nudging his wife.

Philip barely heard them. He leaned toward Alice, adrenaline spiking as it always did when they verbally sparred. He was quickly coming to crave their spats. He loved to watch her eyes flash and the blood rush to her cheeks, and he couldn't help thinking of all the other ways he could evoke that reaction from her that involved his mouth doing much more than talking.

Alice leaned in as well, hands on her hips and eyes blazing. "Well, I wouldn't have had to blackmail you if you'd seen reason and done the gentlemanly thing in the first place."

"Gentlemanly?" Philip's laughter rang out, and John and Elizabet glanced at each other with raised brows. "First of all, I'm no gentleman and never said otherwise," he said, raising a finger to count off his points. "Secondly, gentleman or no, I certainly have enough honor no' to go around stealing other men's betrothed wives just because they dinna care for the arrangement. And thirdly, given our precarious situation and the somewhat illegal status of our dear friends, I stand firm that the only one seeing any reason in this entire circumstance is *me*."

Alice sucked in an outraged breath. "Why of all the—"

"Alice," Elizabet cut in, leaning into their space to get their attention. "Hello," she said with a smile when Alice finally tore her gaze from him.

Philip blinked at Elizabet, his mind a jumble, until he looked at John, who seemed near to wetting himself with laughter. Philip scowled and sat back.

"Perhaps you could tell us *how* this all came about?"

Elizabet asked.

Alice sucked in a breath for a quick retort and then blew it out again with a slight frown. "Which part?"

"The happy occasion of yer newly wedded bliss," John added gleefully.

Philip glared at him, but that made John's grin wider. He never could grasp the gravity of a situation. Or, more to the point, relished in finding amusement no matter the circumstances. In fact, he was being remarkably restrained in this particular instance. Probably out of respect for Alice. Philip had no doubt he'd be getting an earful once they were alone.

"Well, it was a bit of an accident," Alice said. "Philip decided he needed to guard my door throughout the night but had to step away for a few moments—"

"And if ye had stayed put like I ordered—"

"If you had asked instead of ordered—"

"I did."

"You did *not*."

"Wait a moment," Elizabet interrupted. "How did guarding her door turn into a marriage?"

"Because her ladyship decided she was parched and wandered off because she couldna wait another moment for me to return with something to drink. In doing so, she was nearly attacked."

Elizabet's eyes grew round, and she reached over to grasp her friend's hand. "Were you hurt?"

"No, no, I'm quite all right," Alice assured her. "But the commotion caused a scene, and with Philip there and us obviously sharing the room…"

"We declared ourselves man and wife in front of several witnesses."

John frowned slightly. "It's true, the law does recognize such declarations as legally binding, *if* ye truly intended to be wed. In such a circumstance as yours, there shouldn't be an issue…"

"One of the witnesses was an acquaintance of Alice's father, Lord Morley. And he left not long after."

John nodded in understanding. "Then her family will be informed of the union, irregular as it may be, except they might not be aware of that. Only that their daughter is now wed. So, to go back on it now…"

"Would ruin her," Philip finished.

"Well, cheer up," John said, slapping Philip's knee. "Marriage isna such a hardship. Damn pleasant at times." He gave his wife an exaggerated wink, and she rolled her eyes, though her cheeks flushed pink with pleasure.

A servant entered and nodded at Elizabet, who stood with a smile. "Your chamber is ready." She glanced at John, who gave her an almost imperceptible nod of his head. "Alice, how about we get you settled and leave these men to themselves for a bit?"

Alice glanced at Philip and again, that warm spot in his heart glowed at her apparent need to look to him first. He wasn't sure why. It certainly wasn't because she wanted his approval or permission. Perhaps she merely wanted to know what he preferred her to do. So she could do the opposite.

His lips twitched at the thought, and he followed John's example and nodded. Her eyes narrowed slightly, as if she'd just realized what she'd done, but she followed Elizabet out of the room willingly enough.

He watched her until she was out of sight and then turned to find that John had been watching him, eyebrow cocked in either amusement or confusion. Or maybe both.

"So. Tell me how marriage is treating you," he said. Then he burst into laughter.

Philip groaned. "I need another drink."

Chapter Twelve

Elizabet led Alice into a sparse but comfortable chamber and sat down on the bed. "All right. Now tell me what's really going on."

Alice glanced at her in surprise. "We told you all."

"Why would you run from home? Was the man your parents chose so horrible?"

Alice sighed and sank down next to her friend. "In some ways. Not like Mr. Ramsay, of course," she said with a fine shudder. "But horrible all the same. His age I might have been able to deal with, although the thought of him touching me still makes me shudder. But I would have been his fourth wife. Three predecessors and no heir. Three dead predecessors, I should say. All died within a few years of marrying him and none from natural causes. All rather convenient accidents. And the comments he'd make when there was no one else to hear..." A fine tremble ran through her, and she tried to shake it off. "There's no real evidence he's done aught amiss. But the way he looks at me, the things he says... I'm sure the rumors are all true. Evil lurks within him, I know it."

"Lord Woolsmere?" Elizabet asked in a hushed tone.

"Yes!" She seized Elizabet's hands in her own. "You remember the gossip when you were at court."

"Oh, Alice," Elizabet said. Thankfully, she grasped the horror of the situation. "I remember the whispers when he took his third wife, though I hadn't heard she had died as well. Did you share your fears with your parents?"

"Of course, but they said not to put any stock in such idle gossip. And I must believe that because I know they love me and wouldn't knowingly put me in harm's way. Yet...how could I not be afraid for my life? The old lecher probably can't beget a child, but that wouldn't have stopped him from trying. And there would have been no one to keep him from becoming a widower for a fourth time if I failed to deliver an heir, which I most assuredly would have."

Elizabet squeezed her hand.

"I know that is the way of things," Alice continued, "and truthfully, if he was merely some kindhearted old man who wanted some companionship in his waning years, I don't think I'd have minded. Much. I'd have done my duty. After all, with such a union, a little luck would have seen me a widow sooner than later."

Elizabet gasped but it was quickly followed by a laugh. "Ah, Alice. I've missed you so," she said, leaning in for a hug.

"I've missed you, too, my darling Bess," she said, returning the hug. "I have no one in whom I can confide anymore. Aside from Rose, my maid. But it's not the same."

"I know," Elizabet said, patting her hand. "I'm so happy with John. I never knew I could be so happy. But it can be a bit lonely as well, not having another woman to tell all my darkest secrets to." She smiled and nudged Alice's shoulder with her own. "Sorcha is wonderful, but we still don't know each other all that well." She gave Alice's hand a squeeze. "It's good to see you."

"And you!" Alice said, placing her hand gently on her friend's growing middle. "There is so much more of you to see than I expected."

Elizabet laughed and lovingly caressed her belly. "Yes, this was quite the surprise. Well," she said with a laugh when Alice raised her eyebrows, "perhaps not such a surprise. After all, when one is happily married, I suppose these things tend to happen."

"I suppose," Alice mimicked with a laugh. Then she sobered slightly and took both Elizabet's hands in hers. "I would ask if you were truly happy, but I can see it radiating from you." She pulled her friend into a hug. "And you deserve every bit of it."

"As do you." Elizabet pulled away. "You always used to joke about the man you'd marry, and all your plans to cuckold him. Discreetly, of course." She smiled gently. "And now you are here, running from your supposed grand match and married to my husband's kinsman."

Elizabet searched Alice's face. "You seem happy with your circumstances. But are you? Truly? I know the situation sounds unalterable. But if you are truly unhappy, I'm sure something can be done. Perhaps Malcolm could do something. Divorce is difficult, but possible. Unless someone objected to the union being dissolved, I doubt it has to remain permanent. In fact, if you don't register your union and there is no objection from either of you, no one would be the wiser, I'd think. Although, if Philip did wish to continue, all he'd have to do was produce the witnesses…"

Elizabet sighed. "It's all a bit of a muddle that I don't truly understand. Irregular marriages happen, of course, but not so often as you'd think. And there is a great deal of disapproval from many quarters. If you hadn't declared yourselves wed in front of quite so many people, and then very obviously spent the night together…"

Alice waved that off. "Nothing has happened between us. Yet." She smiled briefly and then shrugged. "I suppose as long as I stay here, all would be well should we choose to go our separate ways. But back home, they've surely been told by now that I am wed. Or at least that I was observed spending the night alone in a room with a man I called husband. With Mr. Craven there to witness it all... If I were to return home, without a husband... Well, short of appearing as a widow with Philip's body in tow, no one would ever receive me again. You know how the court is. Everyone looks the other way as long as one is discreet. Causing a scene with your paramour in front of an entire inn of curious onlookers isn't what one would call ideal."

Elizabet gave her a gentle smile. "No, not exactly. But, you do have the option of staying here and dissolving the union. Short of rounding up the witnesses who were at the inn that night, there is precious little anyone could do to prove anything."

"True."

"But?" Elizabet asked.

"I don't know. We fight constantly. The man is insufferable. Arrogant. Demanding. Rigid. And fussy. Did you know he repacked my entire trunk on the ship? Folded everything neatly as could be because he couldn't stand to see the clothing tossed into the trunk with no order. He packs his saddlebags the same way. Everything has to be just so. It's aggravating. Even more so when it comes to making a decision to do something, because every action must be scrutinized and examined repeatedly before he makes a move. It's exhausting. *And* he expects me to obey his every word without question."

"You've just described most men. Certainly those in this neck of the woods."

Alice laughed and then shrugged. "There's something

about him, Bess."

"Is that something worth staying married for?"

Alice paused for a moment, thinking back over everything Philip had said and done. The way he looked at her, touched her, made her feel.

"I think so." She sighed. "But I have to convince *him*."

Elizabet pulled her into another hug. "Then congratulations, my dearest friend. And good luck convincing a MacGregor to change his mind. But if anyone can do it, you can."

"I hope so, Bess. I hope so."

. . .

"Marriage agrees with ye," John said, grinning when Philip scowled at him.

"It's no' like I had much choice in the matter."

"Aye, ye did."

When Philip raised a brow, John repeated it. "Ye did. Though I'll grant ye, the situation was a bit more complicated as an acquaintance of her family was present. But the lady seems happy with the arrangement. Why are ye so against it?"

"Do ye really need to ask me that? She's the daughter of Lord Morley. My parents, rest their souls, were good people with a bit o' land to their names, but none so much as to put me within rights to marry a lady. Even if that werena the case, I never wanted to marry."

John waved that away. "Neither did I. Sometimes circumstances change."

"And sometimes they don't."

John shrugged. "Well, the crux of the matter is that the lady's family has most likely been informed of their daughter's new status. So, if ye dinna wish to bring shame on the lady, then the arrangement must stand, correct?"

"Aye," Philip said, narrowing his eyes.

"So, why be such a surly bastard about it?"

That startled an amused snort out of Philip. Leave it to John to say exactly what he thought. "Because, the lady didna choose me. No' really. She had no intention of finding herself wed to anyone, let alone the likes of me. In fact, she went to great lengths to avoid a marriage to a man she didna want."

"Have ye asked her what she wants now?"

Philip snorted again. "There's no escaping listening to what the woman wants. She's no' shy about speaking her mind."

"Well, then."

"She doesna ken what she really wants. She's impetuous and bullheaded. Never met a rule she didna wish to break. Hell, she's probably saying yes only because I'm sayin' no. She lives to contradict my every wish and command."

"Ye've just described most women I've come across."

Philip snorted but shook his head. "Right now, being with me feels adventurous. The men she's used to are...different. Genteel and bored and like to play games. I'm no' sure she understands this isna a game to me. And what happens several months, or even years from now, when she decides she's had enough of the game?"

"Then, I suppose ye go yer separate ways. Ye wouldna be the first to do so."

Philip frowned at that. If their union was never registered, assuming their split was amicable, there really wouldn't be too much fuss. Even if their union was registered, divorce was a possibility, unlike with their sovereign neighbor to the south. Though it was not one many would undertake.

Truthfully, the thought of remaining married to Alice, and all that would entail, was more enticing than he cared to admit to his kinsman. They had little choice in the matter, unless he wished to send Alice back to her family in disgrace. While sending her away held a great deal of appeal, he'd never do such a thing. And keeping her by his side held more temptation.

He shoved those thoughts aside. "There are other matters that must be discussed."

John's amusement faded, and he nodded, glancing toward the door through which the women had disappeared. "Aye. That wee bastard Ramsay."

Philip nodded as well. "If Alice's family is informed where she is, and who she is with, I dinna think it will be long before Ramsay hears. While I dinna think ye'll be connected to all this, it may give Ramsay the excuse he's been wanting to march on Glenlyon."

"Aye," John said, sitting back with a sigh. "I doubt such an action will be sanctioned by anyone, particularly the king. There are other ways to bring an errant daughter home, so Ramsay willna be able to use Lady Alice as an excuse. Then again, I dinna think that he cares overly much about the legality of his actions. He most likely willna wait to gain permission, preferring to take action and ask for forgiveness later."

"I took every precaution to keep my final destination secret. However…"

John nodded. "However, Ramsay is fully aware of yer connection to me, as ye were at my side when we fought last."

"Aye. And when he hears Alice is with me…"

"He'll assume she's going to Elizabet."

Philip's frown deepened. "He doesna ken the location of Kirkenroch."

"True. But I dinna think he has the resources to take on Glenlyon directly. And Kirkenroch isna so far removed from Glenlyon that it couldna be found if someone were searching hard enough. We've taken care to hire only trusted clansmen to work on the repairs, but it's no' really a secret that we're here. At least in the village."

"We need to take care. Place extra men on guard. Perhaps increase the number of scouts."

John nodded and then his countenance lightened. He sucked in a deep breath and stood. "Aye, we'll take extra precautions. But in the meantime, I believe ye have a new wife waiting for ye in yer chambers."

Philip scowled at his kinsman, and John laughed and clapped him on the shoulder. "Come on, Cousin. Go and straighten out matters with yer wife. Talk of war can wait."

Philip couldn't help but laugh at that. "Not if ye wish me to have a serious discussion about the state of our relationship. War is what it'll be."

"Better get to it then," John said with a wink.

Philip excused himself and made his way upstairs, determination and excitement rushing through him. Never had a soldier been less prepared, yet strangely eager, for battle.

He entered their chamber to find Alice staring out the window at the scene below. She didn't say anything but turned to give him a brief look and then resumed watching out the window. He moved to her side to see what captivated her attention.

The sun was setting over the hills that surrounded Kirkenroch. A hint of the loch which lay near Glenlyon could just be seen over the horizon. The setting rays highlighted the rich colors of the countryside, making the landscape seem almost dreamlike.

"It's beautiful, isn't it?" she asked softly.

"Aye, 'tis."

"So different from London."

"Too different?" he asked, not sure he wanted to hear the answer.

She looked up at him then and gave him a soft smile. "Yes. But that is a good thing." She looked back out the window. "It's peaceful here. So beautiful it makes my heart hurt. It's… real." Her brow furrowed slightly. "London…everything is all about appearances. What was beneath the surface was rarely what one saw. If there was anything there at all. Here… it seems…" She shrugged and gave a little sheepish laugh. "Pure, I suppose. Does that make sense?"

"Aye." It was exactly how he felt about his home. He stepped closer, so her back was nearly pressed against his chest but for the whisper of breath between them. He lightly rested his hands on her upper arms, and she leaned back against him without hesitation. They remained that way, watching the sun drop behind the hills.

He'd wrestled with what he'd say to her. Whether he'd try to get her to stay or go. Whether he wanted her to stay or go. What would be best for them both. For her. He still didn't know the answer.

But he knew, at that exact moment, he wanted her. Had wanted her since the moment he'd seen her twirling in that sparkling ballroom a lifetime ago. And it seemed, for better or worse, their paths were entwined. So why did he keep fighting it? She was already his, in name at least. He merely needed to take that last step.

If she willed it.

He turned her in his arms, brushed her curls from her face. "Do ye wish to be my wife?"

Chapter Thirteen

Alice frowned slightly at the question. Philip stared down at her, his eyes almost daring her to say no.

"I *am* your wife."

He shook his head and stepped back. "By law, what matters most is consent. So, our union might be legal by the letter of the law. But in my mind, intent matters just as much. Ye werena intending to be my wife forever. Ye simply wished to keep yer reputation intact. As did I. So, I dinna care what the rest of the world thinks. I care what you think. No one is here now. Just us. And no one else matters but us."

Alice's heart beat so hard it was near pain. "And the witnesses?"

Philip waved a hand. "If ye wished to return home, there are ways to do so without spoiling yer reputation. Ye've seen the Lady Elizabet. Assured yerself that she is happy and well. Ye've seen how we live. How ye'd live if ye stayed among us. Ye've seen enough to know what ye'd be agreeing to if ye chose to stay. What ye'd be leaving if ye chose to go."

She raised an eyebrow. "I thought we had no other

choices."

His lips twitched in a ghost of a smile. "I didna say they were good choices. Yer family has been informed of our union. English law likely willna acknowledge it. But ye can return home a widow. None will look too closely at yer tale, I'm sure. As long as I stayed away from court, stayed out of England."

"You would do that for me? Exile yourself?"

"If ye wished to return home, aye."

Alice pretended to think about it for a moment. That he would offer something like that made her throat burn with unshed tears. However, she didn't want to betray such emotion, so she smiled instead. "A widow, *hmm*?"

His own lips twitched, and something told her she hadn't fooled him for a moment.

"Aye," he said, stepping closer, his eyes turning a dark shade of blue that had her mesmerized. "Or ye can choose to stay. Here, with me. And so I'm askin', *do ye wish to remain my wife?*"

Alice tried to calm her breathing. Not betray the emotions threatening to erupt. "And what would happen if I say yes?"

He gave her a predatory smile, one that filled her with an overwhelming excitement. And a healthy touch of fear. That look. It was dangerous. Thrilling. He was a hunter surveying his prey. If one so willing could be called prey.

"Then, mistress, as yer chosen husband, I'd take ye to my bed."

Alice's lungs burned with a sudden lack of oxygen, and she tried to suck in air past her rapidly beating heart. His lips hinted at a smile, as if he knew exactly what she was feeling. Maybe he did. His own breathing had sped as he watched her every movement. His hands clenched into fists at his sides. Like he wanted to reach out and touch her. But wouldn't. Until she gave him her answer.

That he gave her the choice meant more to her than she'd ever be able to articulate. She'd been raised to do her duty. Follow her parents' wishes without hesitation. And she'd been prepared, despite being unwilling. Had the man they'd chosen not been more likely to murder her than leave her a young and wealthy widow… Leaving home had been the first choice she'd made for herself. But it wasn't a choice she'd been freely given. She fully believed she'd had no choice if she wanted to live. And she'd been prepared to accept whatever consequences came of her actions. Even if it meant a life of lonely exile. But one glance at the Highland warrior now before her had shown her how different her life could be. He exuded an air about him she'd never encountered before. And she wanted to bask in it. It was more than a physical attraction, though that was so strong it was taking everything she had not to throw herself into his arms.

She'd wanted him from the moment she'd seen him at the ball. He'd been watching her with those heated eyes—his warrior's body lithe and strong and maddeningly tempting. But it was more than that. Despite their differences, she felt safe in his company. Protected, cherished even. They might argue with every other breath. And he might not always follow her counsel or wishes. But he listened. She was more than a pretty conquest to parade around. He saw the real her. He might not always approve. But he cared enough to look.

"There are still things to discuss," she said.

"Oh, aye. Many things." His smile grew wider. "Ye needna fash I'll expect ye to suddenly become a compliant, obedient, docile creature who'll never give me a day o' worry. I fully expect ye to turn my hair gray within a year from yer incessant nagging and arguments."

She couldn't hold back a smile. "Well then, in that case… take me to your bed, my lord."

He didn't wait for her to ask twice.

She wore the simplest gown she owned, yet Philip's fingers still tangled in her laces. But when she finally stepped from the last petticoat, the look in his eyes made every tug and knot worth it.

"My God," he breathed.

"Are you giving thanks or praying to be saved?"

He laughed and pulled her close. "I think I shall be giving thanks for this moment for the rest of my days. Whatever else ye may be, ye wee vixen, ye're more beautiful than anyone I've ever seen."

His obvious appreciation burned away some of the nervousness that lingered, and she tugged at his shirt, wanting to see what she'd caught bare glimpses of before. He dragged his shirt over his head and kicked off his boots so he stood before her in nothing but his kilt. Alice explored his chest, learning every line and plane.

"It's a pity you have to keep this covered all day," she murmured, leaning down to press a kiss right above his heart.

"Oh aye?" he said with a low chuckle. "Ye dinna think I'd be a bit of a spectacle wandering about without a stitch of clothing on?"

"*Hmm*, perhaps you are right," she said, kissing the side of his neck.

He shrugged. "I dinna think I'd ever live to see the day ye'd admit that. I can die a happy man now."

"Not yet you can't," she said, running her hands down his chest. "But you are right about being a spectacle. Crowds would come for miles. I suppose I should keep you all to myself then."

He threaded his hand through her hair, lightly grasping a handful at the nape of her neck to tilt her face up to him. He cupped her cheek with his other hand and lightly brushed his lips across hers. "As long as ye're locked in the room with me, I'll be ye're willing prisoner."

He trailed his mouth across her skin, his lips barely touching, until a little moan of frustration escaped her. He smiled and moved back to her lips, this time taking a long, deep taste of her.

He moved to the sensitive skin of her neck, and she trembled against him. He scooped her up and carried her to the bed, laying her down gently before dropping his kilt. Alice's eyes devoured him. He took his time joining her on the bed, letting her look her fill.

She reached for him with greedy hands, and he chuckled again as he took her in his arms.

"You know," she said, her voice coming out in a breathy gasp, "this doesn't mean I forgive you for going back on your word to bring me to Elizabet."

He nipped at her collarbone, his tongue darting out to taste the hollow of her throat.

"And I dinna forgive ye for blackmailing me to bring ye in the first place."

Alice dragged him back to her mouth. "As long as we're clear on those points." Her hands ran over the taut muscles in his back, reaching down so she could explore all of him.

"Verra clear," he said, arching against her. She gasped, and he returned to kissing his way down her body. Her hands gripped his hair, trying to keep him captive in each new spot he kissed.

"I still find you aggravating," she said, writhing against him.

"As I do you." His mouth brushed against her breasts, and she lost the ability to speak.

"We'll probably never agree on anything," she finally managed to say.

"We seem to be fairly agreeable right now," he said, his hand dipping lower.

"Oh, aye," she said, her words lost in the low moan that

escaped her throat.

He chuckled and rolled her beneath him. She clung to him, wrapping her arms around him. Whatever other point she was going to make disappeared from her mind. She couldn't focus on anything but the feel of his hands, the touch of his mouth. Even the brief moment of pain when he entered her dissolved into a delicious tension that built and built until she didn't know where she began and he ended. She wanted it to go on forever. No more fighting, no more trying to prove who was right or who'd done what to whom first. Just this, their bodies dancing together—for once in perfect harmony.

When the momentum finally reached its peak, she clung to him, his name almost a sob on her lips as wave after wave of intense pleasure washed over her. His rhythm faltered and then he joined her, her name wrung from his lips like a blessing. Or a curse. Perhaps it was both. For she felt the same. No matter how this journey had started, they had taken an irrevocable turn. One that both terrified her and filled her with hope.

But for that one moment, as they lay together, entwined in the dark, she focused on the hope.

• • •

Philip wrapped his arms tighter about Alice and snuggled in to her neck, breathing in the fresh, soft scent of her. They sat curled up on the stone bench near the window so Alice could watch the sunrise. She couldn't seem to get enough of watching the world outside their window. That boded well, he supposed, as she would be happier if she loved her new home.

Alice stiffened, and he looked down at her, concern spiking through him.

"What is it?" he asked.

"There, on the road leading to the gates." She pointed

and leaned closer to the glass, trying to see better. "A rider."

Philip stood. "Two riders. One horse." And they were traveling as fast as the poor animal could carry them. He dressed quickly, and Alice followed suit. They passed a maid who had been sent up to get them as they rushed downstairs and into the great hall.

"Rose!" Alice exclaimed. Her lady's maid rushed to her, and Alice wrapped her arms around the trembling girl.

"William?" Philip asked, frowning at his young kinsman. "What is wrong? What are ye doing here?"

"And why are you with him?" Alice added, looking at Rose.

John's grave face put more fear in Philip than anything else could. For his jovial cousin to look so dour, something terrible must have occurred. And there was only one thing Philip could think of that would put that look on his face.

"Ramsay."

John nodded, and William put down the cup he'd just drained. "He willna be far behind us. A day at the most. We rode as fast as we could but I wasna able to get away as quickly as I'd hoped. And with the horse carrying the both of us…"

Philip clapped his hand on Will's shoulder. "Ye did well, lad."

"But how did the two of you come to be together?" Alice asked, frowning at her maid. "I left you on the docks at Dover. You were supposed to have returned to my parents."

"I'd planned to, my lady. But then—"

"I took her prisoner," Will said, with a tone that suggested he'd been suffering for his actions ever since.

"You did *what*?" Alice asked, taking a threatening step closer.

"It was a misunderstanding—" he started before Rose cut in.

"Because you jumped to conclusions, and rather than

wait two minutes for me to explain, you trussed me up and hauled me off for questioning. Thinking I was a spy for Ramsay!"

"What?" Alice gasped.

"Oh, for the thousandth time, woman, I'm sorry. Ye have no idea how sorry. It was the worst mistake I've ever made in my entire life. And ye've been making me pay for it for weeks now."

"As well you should be! Just because you were off playing spy doesn't mean the rest of us weren't just trying to mind our own business. And then you had to drag me into all of this, when I had strict orders from my lady—"

"Must we go over all this again?" William said, rubbing his face. "At this point, madam, I'd sell my soul to the devil himself if it meant I could undo what I did, but I cannae do that, so ye're just going to have to learn to forgive me or get on with killing me, because I'd rather die a swift death by yer blade than listen to ye naggin' me about it for the rest of my life."

"I'd be glad to oblige, but you took my dagger!"

"Then I'll gladly give ye my own!"

"That's not what you said a few hours ago when I tried to take it from you."

William opened his mouth to respond, but Philip put himself between them. "Now, I'm sure that's a fascinating story, but as long as the lass hasna been hurt in any way…" He looked at Rose with a cocked eyebrow, and she begrudgingly shook her head, though her eyes narrowed at Will.

Philip nodded. "Well then, I say for the moment we let the matter drop and send these two to rest and refresh themselves. They've had an arduous journey in order to bring us this news. We need to use it to our advantage. All else can wait until after Ramsay has been dealt with."

Alice didn't look like she wanted to let the matter drop,

but even she couldn't argue with the need to fortify themselves against the coming attack.

She bundled up her maid and took her upstairs to get settled in the small chamber off their own, while Philip and John took Will into the kitchens to feed the lad and glean whatever information they could.

"I truly am that sorry about the lass, Philip, I swear it…"

"Pay it no mind, Will. For the moment, anyway. There's more important matters to discuss."

Will nodded and took another bracing drink of ale.

John pulled up a stool and sat down. "I'd love to know how the maid plays into all this, but for now," he said, holding his hand up against the immediate defensiveness on Will's face, "just tell us the relevant information on Ramsay. How far away is he? How many men with him? Do you know what he is planning?"

Will told them all he knew, from the moment he'd left Philip at the docks, to when he'd rejoined Ramsay's men in his disguise as one of them, to the moment he'd managed to break away from them in the dead of night just a few hours before.

Philip and John listened with growing concern.

"We haven't much time then," Philip said.

"Nay, my laird," Will said. "A day or two at most. Perhaps less if he's discovered my deception."

John called a lad in and sent him scurrying off to Glenlyon as fast as he could go. Then he turned back to them. "Thank you, Will," John said, clapping both hands on his shoulders. "Ye've given us a chance to prepare a defense. One we didn't have last time. Let's not waste it!"

The rest of that day was spent in a flurry of activity. Every possible entry point was fortified. Every possible precaution was taken. And it still didn't feel enough.

Philip and Alice tried to get some sleep, but the most they managed was a few fitful hours of dozing before they gave up and returned to the window. They sat on the large window seat together, wrapped in a warm fur, and watched through the night for any sign of Ramsay.

Toward dawn, they spotted a lone rider in the distance, galloping like hell itself was on his heels.

They were already dressed. But Philip paused to gather Alice to him and give her a long, lingering kiss. When they pulled apart, she gazed up into his eyes, neither one saying anything.

Then he took her hand and led her below.

"He's here," Philip said, not making it a question. John nodded. "Spotted a few miles away with a large group of men. He marches on Malcolm."

What men were at the manor were already scurrying to and fro, preparing to ride out.

"He attacks Glenlyon?" Philip asked, somehow both surprised and not. "He's a reckless lunatic, but I never believed he'd be so mad as to attack The Lion in his own lair."

John strapped his sword to his hip. "Aye, well I wouldna be surprised by anything that bastard did." He caught Philip's gaze. "But it ends today."

Philip nodded. "Agreed." Then he looked at Alice, whose face had grown so pale it was nearly bloodless. Still, he was pleased to see she was steady on her feet, her arm around Elizabet's waist.

"You're leaving?" Alice asked. She held her head high, though he could see the doubt and fear in her eyes.

He glanced at John, who nodded. "We dinna have many men here," John said, "though we must send who we can to Glenlyon to help rout the bastard. But we'll no' leave ye undefended. Half our men will stay, as will young William. I'll need ye to help me lead our men," he said to a startled-looking William, who nonetheless nodded solemnly at the charge he was given.

Then John went to stand by his wife. "And I'll stay to guard ye."

The love that shown from Elizabet's face was almost painful to behold. She reached up to touch her husband's cheek. And then she firmly shook her head.

"You'll do no such thing."

"Elizabet," John said.

"Malcolm needs you," she said.

"Do ye truly think I'll be any good to him at all when my mind is here with you and our babe?" he asked, placing his hand over her belly. "Ramsay is here for you. I'll no' leave yer side until he's captured or dead."

Alice met Philip's gaze, questioning. He wrapped his arms about her. Before he could tell her that he'd stay by her side as well, she sucked in a deep breath, a fine tremor running through her body as she pulled away.

"You must go," she said.

He frowned, his eyes searching her face for any sign of what she was truly thinking.

"Ye dinna wish me to stay with ye?" he asked, reaching up to brush her cheek.

She leaned in to his hand for a brief moment before straightening her spine and stepping away from him. "We'll be fine here. We can't deprive Malcolm of both you and John, and John must certainly stay here with Elizabet. They need you at Glenlyon. Ramsay and his men must be stopped before they can make their way here."

Every word she said was the truth, but it still felt like a rejection. One that stung much more than he dreamed possible.

But before he could step away, a small smile touched her lips and she took his face in her hands, pulling him down for a kiss. One that had his blood roaring—that held the promise of so much more.

She pulled away, but only far enough so she could bring his forehead down to hers. "You come back to me." Her hands trembled on his cheeks, but she took a deep breath and stepped back. "We still have much to discuss, husband."

He laughed. "Aye, wife. That we do."

John motioned for him to follow, and he nodded. He pulled Alice close once more and kissed her hard and fast.

"Stay hidden," he said, fear spiking through him at the thought of Alice left to her own devices. "Listen to John. Take Elizabet, hide in one of the inner chambers, lock the door, and whatever ye do, stay there. No matter what."

"I'll be fine, real—"

"No." He took her chin in his fingers and made sure she was looking right in his eyes. "Promise me. For once, do as I say. Go to our chamber, lock the door, and dinna leave for any reason. Do ye understand?"

She blinked at him, and her jaw clenched beneath his fingers.

He closed his eyes briefly and prayed for patience. Losing his temper would simply make her dig in her heels, and this was too important. She might feel safe behind these thick stone walls, but he'd seen sturdier places crumble.

"I ken well enough what I'm asking of ye. Doing as ye're told willna ever be something ye're good at, I think." He gave her a faint smile, and some of the tension eased from her. "But in this instance, ye must listen, Alice. And obey. Do not leave this house. Aye?"

She nodded. "I will stay put and be right here waiting for you when you return."

He stared at her, wishing he actually believed that.

"Philip," John called.

He glanced over his shoulder at his waiting kinsman and nodded. Then he grasped Alice by the back of the neck, pressed a kiss to her forehead, and turned on his heel, resisting the urge to look over his shoulder.

She'd hide. She'd be safe. And she'd be waiting when he returned.

To believe anything else was unthinkable.

Chapter Fourteen

Alice watched Philip ride out with a heavy heart. After all they'd been through, they'd finally seemed to come to an understanding. Or…perhaps they hadn't. They still had so much to discuss. They seemed so different. She knew that hardly mattered when it came to marriage but, if she wanted a happy marriage, that rare and elusive thing, then working out their differences mattered a great deal. And if he never came back…

She sucked in a breath, swallowed past the sudden lump in her throat, and turned to find Elizabet. There was a great deal to do to make sure those who were sheltering in the house would be protected.

John mobilized the men who'd stayed behind. William was overseeing moving what women and children were in the house up to one of the inner chambers. Thankfully, there were not more of them. But enough.

Rose was on his heels, berating him for something or other. Given the pained expression on his face, he'd heard more than an earful of her ire already. Alice would have to ask her maid for more details on what had transpired between them on the journey to Kirkenroch.

Alice and Philip's chamber had a small dressing chamber behind it that had only one small window set high in the wall and was cleverly disguised behind a tapestry. The women and children were ushered in there and hidden away.

When John tried to get Elizabet to go inside, however, he ran into some resistance.

"I can do more good out here," she said, grabbing another old petticoat that they had begun shredding for bandages.

"Elizabet, I canna stay here to guard ye. I must make sure the men are ready should Ramsay attack."

"I'm not asking you to. Go and do as you must," she said with a sweet smile.

Alice and Rose exchanged a glance and turned to hide their smiles.

"I'll stay and watch over them, my lord," William offered. "Should we come under attack, I'll make sure they are well hidden before any danger descends."

John hesitated but finally nodded. "I'll be back as soon as I can," he said to his wife, giving her a quick kiss.

Elizabet watched him walk out and then sank onto the bed with a pained sigh. Alice rushed to her side.

"Bess, are you all right? Is it the babe?"

Elizabet tried to wave her off, but she kept a hand pressed to her belly. "I'm fine. A few small pains, is all. It's nothing."

Alice frowned and rested her hand against her friend's belly. She didn't seem to be in the type of pain that Alice had heard accompanied childbirth, not that she'd ever seen it herself. But she didn't think Elizabet should be experiencing pains this early. She still had a couple months to go before the babe was due. Perhaps the stress of the situation was causing it.

She watched Elizabet closely, but aside from a few twinges

that made her wince, she did seem to be relatively all right.

They prepared bandages until there were no more to prepare, under the watchful eye of William, who took his guard duties very seriously. The sun climbed higher in the sky. But no word came from Glenlyon. Surely they should have heard something by now.

Alice had finally gotten Elizabet to eat a small bite of food, though she did little more than nibble a piece of bread and nurse a cup of ale.

"Damn," she muttered. Alice looked at her in shock. She didn't think she'd ever heard her friend utter such a word in her life.

Elizabet was brushing at a wet spot on the front of her gown. "I'm afraid I'm growing clumsier by the day," she said. She hauled herself out of her chair with a sigh. "I'm going to change."

William frowned. "My lord said that no one was to leave this chamber, my lady."

"I am going just to the end of the hall. I'll be only a moment."

William glanced back and forth between Elizabet's retreating back and the hidden door behind the tapestry. He'd been charged with protecting both, something that Elizabet was making impossible. He focused his gaze on Alice, and it was clear he wanted her to side with him and get Elizabet back into the dressing room. And with the promise to Philip ringing in her head, Alice knew she should follow his wishes.

But the distress on Elizabet's face pulled at her heart. Especially with the periodic signs of pain she tried unsuccessfully to hide. If the babe were to be born now, it would surely die. With the stress of the coming confrontation and the monster who'd been stalking her and John fighting his way to their door, Alice would do anything to keep her friend calm.

"I'll go with her," Alice said. "I'll make sure she hurries."

William's frown darkened at that. "Forgive me, my lady, but both of you should be in with the other women. I really must insist…"

But Elizabet was already out of the door, muttering about being uncomfortable enough without being wet, too.

"I'll look after her," Alice promised, following her friend. "We'll make all haste."

To their credit, they had Elizabet changed and in a clean gown in a few minutes. They were nearly to the door to go back to Alice's chamber when they heard a shout from outside. Both women flew to the window. But their vantage point didn't offer a view of what was going on. The sound of wood splintering downstairs did, however.

"Was that the door?" Alice asked.

Shouts and metal clashing with metal rang through the house.

Elizabet's face paled, and Alice reached over to take hold of her arm. "We need to get to the dressing chamber. Quickly," she said, steering Elizabet to the door.

"Yes," she said. But Elizabet had taken only a few steps when she doubled over with a pained cry.

"Elizabet!"

Alice wrapped an arm around her friend and supported as much of her weight as she could. She had to get her to the hidden chamber before the shouts downstairs moved any closer. Alice helped her into the hallway. But they were too late.

Two men stumbled to the top of the stairs, and Alice and Elizabet froze.

One of them pointed to Elizabet and gave her a disturbing smile before loosing a roar. "She's here, my lord!" he shouted over his shoulder. Then they both ran for the women, but they didn't get far.

William stepped out of Alice's chamber with a shout and felled one of their assailants. The other raised his sword, and William swung his to deflect. A vase came sailing out of the chamber's doorway, crashing into William's opponent and distracting him long enough for William to turn and look at Alice and Elizabet. He shouted one word.

"Run!"

Terror flooded through her, rooting Alice to the floor until Rose came flying out of the chamber, sword in hand.

"We need to go, my lady. Now!"

She thrust a dagger into Alice's hand and then looped an arm around Elizabet's waist.

Elizabet pointed at the far end of the hall, closest to her bedchamber. "The stairs there lead to the old kitchens. They are shut off for now, but we can get out of the house through the back."

Alice pushed aside the guilt that pricked at her. If she had listened to Philip, if she had made Elizabet go into the chamber instead of allowing her to leave the safety of the hidden room, she wouldn't be dragging her friend through the ruins of an old kitchen on the run from a madman.

Maybe she could find a place here to hide. Surely staying in the house would be safer than running into the woods. But a quick glance around didn't offer any hope of adequate concealment.

More shouts and clashing steel spurred them out the door. They stayed plastered to the wall of the house while Alice took a moment to gauge their surroundings. She couldn't see the front of the house, but from the sound of things the main bulk of the fighting had moved inside.

Alice sent up a quick prayer for the hiding women and children. And for themselves. Then she took up her position on Elizabet's other side and she and Rose half supported, half dragged Elizabet into the small copse of woods at the back of the manor.

They hadn't gone far when the unmistakable sound of running footsteps came from behind them. Alice scanned the area, frantic to find a place to hide Elizabet. They couldn't outrun whoever was hunting them. Not with Elizabet in her condition.

The pounding footsteps came closer. More than one set. Terror set her heart to pounding so hard her head swam, but she fought it back. "There!" she said, finally spotting a bramble of bushes and ferns where they could conceal themselves. Or at least Elizabet.

But it was already too late.

Three men entered the clearing. Two men Alice didn't recognize. But the third…

"Ramsay," Elizabet gasped.

His gaze narrowed in on her, the cruelty and hatred emanating from him twisting his face into the visage of a demon.

He took a step closer and stopped, eyes widening when he saw Elizabet's burgeoning belly. He shook his head.

"I'd heard the rumors. That you'd run off with that highwayman scum," he said, nearly spitting out the words. "Your parents, of course, put it out that you'd joined a convent on the Continent. Penance for all your many sins, breaking our engagement not the least among them. Your father would turn over in his grave if he saw you now. Carrying the spawn of the criminal who destroyed his life and sent him to an early death."

"What?" Elizabet gasped.

Ramsay gave her a cruel smile. "Oh yes, I suppose you wouldn't have heard the news, buried away in this Scottish hovel. He died a week ago. Drank himself to death under the shame of his disgrace and debtors beating down his door. Add that to your list of sins."

Elizabet's face paled even more, and Alice stepped in front of her, raising her dagger.

"If her father felt the need to drown his own sins, that is on him. Elizabet is not the villain here. You are."

Ramsay laughed, and the sound sent an icy shiver down Alice's spine even as it fueled her anger. He obviously didn't see her as a threat. That would change if he dared take one more step in their direction. She spared a quick glance at his men. For the moment, they seemed content to wait for orders from their master and held their positions slightly behind him.

"Lady Alice. I had hoped to find you here. In fact, I wished to thank you. The news of your marriage to a MacGregor heathen was the information I'd been waiting for. I'd wondered—when your rumored engagement was never announced, but your sister's in your stead—if you'd followed in that whore's footsteps and run off," he said, jerking his head at Elizabet.

Alice gasped, sickening terror rushing through her with such force she nearly dropped to her knees.

"Didn't see that one coming, did you?" he asked with a cruel laugh. "I was rather impressed, to tell the truth. Your parents came out of the whole mess spectacularly, putting it about that they'd intended Woolsmere for your sister all along while you'd been promised to some obscure Highland laird. No one believes it, of course, but are too polite to say so, and so everyone saves face and lives happily ever after, eh?"

Alice choked back burning tears. Not Mary. How could her parents do such a thing? Why would Woolsmere accept her sister after Alice's betrayal? *What have I done?* She'd wanted to escape him but would never have sacrificed her sister to do it.

Ramsay ignored her turmoil, acknowledging it with a knowing smirk as he continued spewing his hateful tirade.

"I knew wherever you were, Elizabet would not be far off. And once I dispatch with this traitor, your parents will surely pay a handsome sum for your return. This day is turning out better than I'd hoped," he said to his men, who laughed obligingly.

Fury and guilt flashed through Alice, and she stepped forward, both hands grasping the dagger. This was all her fault. Philip had been right. She should have stayed home and married whom her parents had chosen like a dutiful daughter—no matter the danger or outcome. It should have been her burden alone to bear. Not Mary's. Not Elizabet's. The thought of never having known Philip made her heart ache, but at what cost had her moment of happiness come?

"Where is John?" Elizabet asked, her voice strained.

Ramsay raised a brow. "The last I saw your paramour, he was bleeding on the floor of this ruin you've been living in."

Elizabet gasped and swayed against Rose.

"His mistake was in staying here and not riding to Glenlyon like the rest," Ramsay said, clearly relishing Elizabet's pain. "I knew he'd never leave your side. One of the stable boys was most forthcoming about where he was likely to be. Of course, I slit his throat anyway. Wouldn't do to reward such disloyalty."

"You evil bastard," Alice said, her heart and mind reeling.

"Now, now," he said, his tone placating, though his face had gone a strange mottled shade of red. "Such language doesn't become a lady." Then he waved his hand. "Enough of this. Take care of those two," he said to his men. "Try not to damage Lady Alice too much. But leave the Lady Elizabet. She's mine to punish."

Elizabet put a hand on Alice's arm but dropped it when another pain gripped her. Rose kept one arm firmly about her while the other still gripped the sword. She would need both hands to swing it, if it came to that. Alice prayed it would not. But they were far from the house and, with the fighting going on, she doubted anyone would even hear their screams. They should have stayed put. Should have stayed hidden.

Philip, where are you?

The men advanced, smiling, obviously seeing no threat. And they were probably right. But she'd be damned if she was going to make it easy for them. She tried to force her rising panic down and focus on the enemy before her. She could regret her impulsive decisions later. She needed to do what she could to keep them all alive. And pray help came before it was too late.

One of the men lunged at her, and she slashed out at him, yelling for all she was worth. He apparently hadn't expected her to actually fight him, because he didn't move fast enough, and her dagger slashed through his arm. He grabbed the wound and glared down at his bloodstained fingers.

"You'll pay for that, you bitch," he growled at her.

Her hands trembled, and she gripped the dagger with both hands, ready to try again. But he didn't give her the chance to get her bearings. He rushed her, knocking her off her feet. She went down with a cry, landing hard on her back. But she kept her grip on her dagger even as she tried to scramble away.

Screams came from the other women, and Alice risked a glance. Rose had been backed up against a tree, though she'd managed to bloody her assailant. But the weight of the sword was obviously too much for her. Ramsay stalked Elizabet. By the look on his face, he was enjoying drawing it out, relishing the rising terror in his victim. Elizabet fumbled for the pocket in her skirts, and Alice prayed she'd managed to stash a weapon there.

The man attacking Alice took advantage of her momentary distraction to lunge and straddle her, pinning her down with his weight. He grabbed the wrist holding the dagger.

"No!" Alice shouted, trying to kick at him, even with her legs hampered by her skirts and his crushing weight.

She sat forward and sank her teeth into his hand. The sharp metallic tang of blood and the foul filth of his skin flooded her mouth, and she kept from vomiting by sheer iron will alone.

He bellowed in pain and let go. Her triumph was short-lived. His fist lashed out, catching her full on the cheek, and black spots filled her vision. Shouts rang out in the distance, and she prayed it was help coming and not her suddenly fuddled mind conjuring what she wanted most.

The man snarled down at her and raised his fist again, but the sound of a shot ringing through the clearing distracted him.

Alice looked to where Elizabet had been facing off with Ramsay. Her friend stood pressed against a tree, a pistol in each hand. She'd obviously fired one, as a faint puff of smoke dissipated from its muzzle. She dropped it as Ramsay clutched his side and staggered away from her, spewing rage-filled profanity.

"I'll kill you, you bitch! I'll cut that bastard from your belly and let you watch it die as you bleed out like the miserable cow you are!"

Alice struggled anew, terror for her friend adding strength to her tired muscles. The man atop her cuffed her again, and her ears rang.

From the corner of her eye she caught the glint of the sun on the other pistol in Elizabet's hand. Her friend fired. This time, the bullet found its mark, square in Ramsay's chest. He sank to his knees and then toppled to the ground.

Elizabet dropped the gun and slumped against the tree at her back.

The man atop Alice was momentarily distracted by his leader's defeat, but Alice knew it wouldn't last long. And Ramsay, murderous bastard that he was, had been the only person keeping his men from doing what they pleased to her. She had to strike before he turned his full attention back to her.

She gritted her teeth, redoubled her grip on her blade, and plunged it as hard as she could into the joint between the man's shoulder and neck.

He roared out his pain and surprise, clawing at the dagger still protruding from his neck. Alice pushed at him, trying to dislodge him from atop her. He yanked the dagger out and Alice screamed. She had no weapons left. Nothing but her fists so she pummeled him as well as she could.

Blood poured from his wound, soaking into her gown and splashing on her skin. She shrieked again in rage and despair, trying desperately to escape from the warm sticky liquid drenching her. The man's face paled. His eyes went wide. And he slowly slumped on top of her.

Alice kicked and struggled as his foul breath left his body in one last sigh.

Her momentary relief changed to panic. His dead weight was slowly crushing her, squeezing the air from her body. She twisted and shoved, her desperation growing. Sobs escaped her throat. She tried to hold them back, but overwhelming frustration mixed with panic were more than she could conquer.

Then, his weight was gone. She dragged in a deep breath and blinked through the sunlight at the man who'd taken his place. She couldn't see his face and when he gathered her in his arms she fought against him.

"Alice, stop, lass, it's me," he said. And she finally recognized the familiar touch of Philip's hands on her body, of his chest beneath her cheek, and she collapsed against him, clutching his shirt in her hands.

Another bolt of panic shot through her, and she pushed away from him again, trying to crawl to where she'd last seen her friend.

"Elizabet!"

Chapter Fifteen

Philip lunged after Alice, his heart thudding in his chest with the fear pumping through him. "She's well, lass. She's well."

Alice stilled at that and looked at him with a frown. He pointed to where John was cradling his wife, and Alice sagged, all the fight draining out of her.

"John's alive?" she asked.

He nodded. "Took a wicked blow or two, but aye. He'll live."

"I think her pains have started."

He smoothed her hair from her blood-covered face with trembling hands. "Dinna fash. She'll be taken care of."

"Rose?" she asked, starting again.

"Aye, she's fine. A bit bruised and spittin' angry, but fine. Ye can rest now."

Philip pulled Alice back into his arms. Blood soaked through her dress and covered her skin. His hands frantically checked her for injuries. She winced a few times, but nothing seemed to be fatal.

"Not mine," she said, her voice so low he almost couldn't

hear it. She held her trembling, blood-covered hands out in front of her. "The blood isn't mine. I...I killed him." Her voice choked off on a sob.

"It's all right, love. Shh, *mo cridhe*, it's all right." He held her tightly to him, his chest burning with emotion. He kissed the top of her head. "Ye did what ye had to do. Ye did well. Let it bide, now. I've got ye."

She finally relaxed against him, and he wasted no time in scooping her up in his arms so he could carry her back to the house. He focused on putting one step in front of the other. Nothing more. Because if he thought of how he'd found her... covered in blood with that man atop her...he'd lose his mind.

He didn't even remember running to her side. He'd entered the clearing and saw them and...then he was staring down at the dead man. He didn't even remember pulling the body off her. The only thought in his mind had been getting to her. Saving her. But she'd already saved herself. All the women had done exceptionally well. Surprisingly, considering their condition and the tools they'd had.

But it shouldn't have been necessary. If Alice had simply done what he'd asked...

He shied away from that line of thinking. For the moment, he needed to focus on Alice. He could berate her later. It would be best if he had some time to compose his emotions first. With fear for her and adrenaline from the battle still raging in his blood, he didn't trust himself to speak calmly about the situation. And the last thing he wanted to do was add to her ordeal. Whatever mistakes she'd made, she'd already paid for them tenfold.

But they *would* discuss it. She had to learn she couldn't follow every impulse that came across her mind. This wasn't one of her father's palaces. And men like Ramsay wouldn't stop because of who she was. That lesson, she'd obviously learned.

He held her closer to him and marched straight to their room, calling for a bath to be set up. It was a terrible bother to have the tub brought up and filled with hot water, but she was too soiled to simply wipe down. He wanted to get her clean before she became fully aware again. She'd killed her first man. An experience that could shake the strongest of men. He didn't want her to wake still covered in the man's blood.

John's housekeeper offered to wash Alice and get her situated, but he wasn't going to let her out of his sight again. He carefully bathed her, checking her everywhere for injuries. That bastard had hit her hard enough to blacken her eye, and her cheek would be swollen for a few days. If he'd been alive, Philip would have killed him all over again. Slowly. She also had a bump on her head and various other bruises, but nothing that would leave permanent damage.

Once he had her washed and in a clean shift, he tried to put her in their bed. But she insisted on checking on the other women first. She opened the door to reveal a startled Rose, one arm poised to knock, the other arm full of bundles.

"Rose? What is it?" Alice asked, voice full of concern.

"My pardon, my laird, my lady," she said with a small curtsy and nod to each of them, "but I must beg your permission to leave for a short time. I would never ask, but I have no choice."

Alice frowned but answered, "Of course, you may have as long as you need."

"Thank you, my lady," she said, the relief evident in her voice. She went at once to the small room off the main chamber where she'd been sleeping and began to pack.

"Only please tell me what is wrong," Alice said, following her. "Perhaps I can help."

A worried Elizabet and John entered. "Is Rose here?" Elizabet asked. "The housekeeper said she sat still barely long enough to have her wounds tended and then announced she had to go save William and ran up here."

Philip pointed to the women. Alice asked, "Rose?"

She sighed and glanced up. "William has not yet returned, and there has been no word from him. The search party doesn't know where to look. I do."

"Then tell us," Philip said. "We'll send more men—"

"You can't spare them," she said, adding a "Sir," with wide eyes when she realized who she addressed. "I can find him quicker, with less trouble to the rest of the house."

John strode back to the chamber door and called out to one of the young lads who was always nearby to do his laird's bidding. After a quick exchange the boy ran off, and John came back to the group.

Alice watched with a worried expression as Rose shoved a few more provisions in her saddlebags and checked back through them to make sure she had everything she could possibly need. Food, a few medicines that might be useful, bandages, a flask of whisky.

"Are you sure you wish to do this?" Alice asked her as Elizabet tucked extra supplies into the bags. "At least wait for morning."

"I cannot," Rose said. "He's already been missing for several hours, and he was wounded. He would have returned by now if he could."

Alice and Elizabet exchanged a glance, and Rose jutted her chin in the air. "I know what everyone thinks. But you don't know William as I do. The man is as stubborn as they come and not nearly intelligent enough to give up and die like a normal man. He's out there suffering somewhere. I owe the fool. And so, I'm going to find him and bring him home, so he can suffer in peace."

Her words might have been harsh, but Philip recognized the worry beneath them. Rose and William had been through quite an ordeal on their way to Glenlyon to warn the

MacGregors of Ramsay's imminent appearance. Whatever had gone on between them had bonded them enough that Rose felt the need to go find the missing William, despite her apparent animosity toward him.

As most of the men and women at Glenlyon and Kirkenroch had felt the same way about their partners at some point in their relationships, Philip understood but kept it to himself. He was the last one to be doling out relationship advice. But he could do something to help.

He stepped up and handed Rose a small dagger. She looked at him with surprise but took it readily enough and slipped it into the pocket of her skirt.

"Young Rob is armed as well," John said, nodding to the stable boy who had joined them and who stood, slightly nervous-looking but determined, ready to accompany Rose as she looked for William.

Rose didn't seem to know what to say but finally nodded and murmured her thanks. Elizabet gave her a quick kiss on her cheek and wished her Godspeed before being whisked off to bed by an impatient and disapproving midwife.

Rose gathered her things, and everyone else accompanied her to the courtyard. John pulled young Rob aside for some last-minute instructions, so Rose mounted her horse and nodded at each of them.

"If you're not back by tomorrow, we'll send riders out after you," Alice said. "I understand your wish to find William, but I don't want to lose you as well."

Rose nodded. "I understand. The place he spoke of shouldn't be too far from here. If he's not there then…" She shrugged, and her face paled slightly. Then she straightened her shoulders and gripped the reins. "I'll be back soon. Or will send word," she promised, glancing at Rob.

Then she turned her horse and led it over to where Rob now waited. John saw them to the gate and then hastened to his wife's bed. Alice waited, raising her hand in farewell once more, worry and sadness making her already pale face more drawn. Philip wrapped an arm around her waist.

"She'll find him," he said, leaning down to kiss her cheek.

"How can you be certain?" she asked.

"Because she's as stubborn as you are," he said. He chuckled when Alice glared at him and drew her closer. "And because she loves him, I think."

"Then I pray she finds him quickly."

She and Philip watched until Rose and Rob disappeared over the horizon. The moment they were out of sight, Alice leaned heavily against him, her strength seeming to leave her in a rush.

"There's nothing more we can do for them now," Philip said, sweeping her into his arms again. "I'm taking ye straight to bed."

The fact that she neither protested nor made lewd suggestions sent fresh spikes of worry tearing through him. He brought her straight to their chamber and tucked her into bed.

And then he sat in a chair beside her and watched her chest rise and fall.

He didn't know how long he'd been there when John came in. Long enough for the sun to be setting in the sky and for his eyes to feel as if they were full of sand. He started when John put his hand on his shoulder.

"How is she?" he asked, keeping his voice quiet.

Philip looked back at her. "She'll do, I think. She's got a nasty bump on her head that worries me, and her face will hurt something fearful for a few weeks. But she'll heal. Your lady?"

The ghost of a smile touched John's lips, though his face remained drawn with concern. He gestured to the door and waited until Philip joined him in the room across the hall before continuing.

"She's physically well. The pains have subsided, but the midwife is insisting she stay in bed to be safe. Your lady and her maid defended her well. She wasna injured."

"But?" Philip prompted when John didn't continue.

John sighed and rubbed a hand over his bruised face. "She frets over her father. The man was a criminal whom she's glad to be away from. But he was still her father, after all. I think she hoped to make peace with him someday, and that's no longer possible. And she worries about her mother. I've promised to inquire after her."

"And Ramsay?"

John shook his head, his smile a bit more real this time. "She shot that bastard dead where he stood and, as far as I can tell, isna suffering any qualms over it. I dinna even ken where she got the pistol. But I'll thank every saint in heaven the rest of my days that she had it."

Philip snorted. "I wish we had seen that."

"Aye." He heaved another great sigh. "We lost some good men. And the search parties found no sign of William. There's been no word from either him or Rose yet. The last he was seen, he was being chased by several of Ramsay's men. He led them away from the chamber where the women hid. His actions saved them all, but…" John frowned.

"Take heart," Philip said. "There's still time yet."

John nodded, but there wasn't much hope in his eyes.

He sucked in a deep breath and slowly let it out. "But Glenlyon still stands. Ramsay was too fixated on finding me and Elizabet to waste his time attacking the castle. The men he set to the task were fodder. A diversion while he made his way here." John looked down at his hands. "I thought I was protecting her by staying by her side. Instead, all I did was act as a beacon and led that bastard right to her."

Philip clapped his hand on his cousin's shoulder. "We did

as we felt best. Perhaps ye should have left. And I should have stayed. Perhaps if Alice had stayed put like I'd bid her...if she'd never come at all..." His jaw clenched against the urge to rage and rail at her stubborn impulsiveness. He didn't know what had led to the women being out in the forest, but those who'd hidden in the dressing chamber had been found safe and sound. When he'd opened that door and seen that Alice wasn't there...

He jammed a hand through his hair and paced back and forth in front of the room's hearth.

"The women did well," John reminded him. "Even little Rose. She nearly severed the leg of the man who attacked her. The lass could barely lift the sword, but she put it to good use."

"Aye, but they shouldna have been there in the first place," Philip said, nearly spitting the words out.

Alice...*his* Alice...covered in blood...

He couldn't erase the image from his mind. Finding her in that clearing. Fighting off that man. Covered in blood.

The pent-up emotions of the last few hours were beginning to boil over, and he suddenly had no desire to keep them in.

"She promised me, John. Promised she'd obey this once and stay put. And where do I find her? Out in the bloody woods, fighting off Ramsay and two of his men with naught but a pregnant woman and a maid."

"They had a bit more than that," John reminded him.

"It doesna matter! If she'd listened, she never would have been in danger. How am I supposed to spend my life with a woman who willna listen to reason? I dinna expect her to blindly obey my every whim, but when she is so stubborn and bullheaded and impulsive that I canna even trust her to do what's best to save her own neck? We'll spend our whole lives at each other's throats."

"Ye're wedded and bedded, if I'm no' mistaken," John

said gently, with a touch of his old humor in his voice. "What's done is done. It's naught but yer fear for her talkin' now."

"Maybe so, maybe no'," Philip said. "She'd still be safer in London. She could still return home. Tell everyone I died in the latest attack. She could go back to her old life. She'd probably be happier that way."

"And you?" a voice said behind him. "You could go back to your life as if I never existed? Simple as that?"

Philip spun around to find Alice standing behind him, her hair tumbling down her shoulders, clad in her shift and bare feet, a blanket pulled tight around her. She looked so achingly beautiful he wanted to drop to his knees in front of her and worship her like the goddess she was. But he shoved all that away. They would both be better off if they went their separate ways. Life would be…simpler again. They were too different. They'd proved that over and over. She wasn't suited for this life. She should be wandering marbled palace halls, not fighting for her life in the heather.

Philip let his silence be his answer. Alice nodded, her eyes shining with unshed tears. Her fire had dimmed. That once brilliant light in her eyes that drew him to her despite his better judgment. His heart clenched at that. Fractured a bit more. It would shatter completely when she walked away.

But it was best. He had to believe that.

She visibly pulled herself together and looked at John. "How is Bess?"

"She's well, my lady. Fretting that it was her fault the three of you ended up in the forest."

Alice shook her head. "Philip was right. It was my fault."

His head jerked up, and he started to argue that, though he agreed with her.

But Alice pressed on. "Elizabet wasn't well, wasn't thinking clearly. I wanted to make her happy, but I knew we should stay put. I thought it would be okay. It wasn't. She might have listened to me, but instead I led her right into danger. Danger that wouldn't have been on our doorstep in the first place if it wasn't for me. Ramsay told me he'd followed me. Knew that if I'd run off, I'd run to Elizabet. And now Ramsay has attacked, and my sister is in Woolsmere's clutches. Good men have died, Elizabet and your child may be in danger, Rose and William are God knows where…and now my sister… So many lives that have been and may still be destroyed. And it is all my fault."

She met Philip's gaze, though she almost flinched. "You were right all along. I'm too impulsive. You're too rigid. We'll kill each other inside of a year. Why should we both be miserable over an accidental marriage? If you wish to be dead to me, so be it."

"Alice…"

She turned away from him again to address John. "I do not wish to return home until I have healed. My return will cause enough of a stir without adding a face full of bruises. Perhaps I can stay until Bess has delivered. There should be some months before my sister will wed. I have time, I think. If you'll continue to offer me your hospitality until then…"

"Of course, my lady," John said, with a brief glance at Philip. "Whatever you wish."

She nodded her thanks and then turned back to Philip. "Perhaps it would be best if you returned to Glenlyon. I'm sure they could use the extra hand. If you prefer not, then I'll go. I can return to visit…"

He shook his head. "Ye'll be happier here with the Lady Elizabet. I'll go."

She stared at him a moment, pain shining from her eyes. "Well then." Her voice trembled, and she cleared her throat. "As that is settled, I'll go look in on Elizabet."

Philip nodded, and she turned and walked out as if she were a queen dripping in jewels, instead of a broken girl wrapped in bedsheets.

"Ye're a fool," John said, and the anger in his voice made Philip look at him with surprise.

"I'm trying to do what's best for both of us. She'd never be happy here, with me."

"Oh? And how do ye ken that?"

"Ye've seen us together. We do nothing but fight. She argues every word out of my mouth."

"Aye, and ye both enjoy every second of it."

Philip ignored that, mostly because he didn't want to admit that his cousin was right. "I canna trust her. She gave me her word…"

"Aye, and she did her best to keep it. Elizabet said that Alice tried to prevent her from leaving the safety of that room, but when she pressed, Alice accompanied her to hurry her along. And ye complain enough about her impulsive nature, but her ability to act without questioning every action is what saved them today."

"That may not always be the case. Even if it were, even if our very natures werena at complete odds, she's no' suited for life here."

"Oh? And why is that? My wife has done wonderfully. As has the Lady Sorcha."

"The Lady Sorcha is wife to our laird and lives in a fine castle, and ye've given yer lady this manor to live in."

John snorted. "Aye, a crumbling pile of stone that is barely habitable."

"Now. But someday soon it will be a fine manor again and yer lady can live her days in comfort. What have I to offer? I've no vast estates to inherit."

"Ye have land. That's a fair sight better than nothing."

"No' by much. She's the daughter of an earl. She has no place here as the wife of a beleaguered laird of a mound of dirt with no' even a home on it to rest her head."

"Then build her one. Maybe ye should let her judge where her place is."

Philip shook his head. "She never meant for any of this to happen. She wanted only to see her friend. Our marriage is no marriage. And with Ramsay's attack, it would be reasonable to assume I'd died. She can go back to her own life where she'll be pampered and spoiled, and I can…"

"Aye? Ye can what?"

Philip shook his head. "It doesna matter." He stood and gathered his sword and coat. "I'll take my leave now. I dinna wish to inflict my presence on her further. If…" He hesitated to say it. Best to make a clean break. But he didn't want to abandon her entirely. "If she has need of anything…"

"I ken where ye'll be."

Philip nodded and marched out, forcing himself to walk away before he gave in to the voice screaming in his head to turn around.

It was for the best. No matter how wrong it felt.

Chapter Sixteen

Alice pulled the blanket tighter and lay against the pillows with Elizabet.

"Are you sure this is what you really want?" Elizabet asked her.

"It's what he wants. I can't fight him anymore. And besides, he's been right about everything. Don't you dare tell him that." She shrugged. "But he's right about this, too."

"What else has he been right about?"

"He said that Ramsay was watching me. That me insisting on finding you would lead Ramsay right to you. I didn't want to listen. But he was right." She laid her head on Bess's shoulder. "I'm so sorry, Bess. All of this is my fault. He never would have found you if it wasn't for me."

"Hush. The man was insane. He would have found me eventually. I'm glad it happened now, before the babe was born." Her hand curled protectively over her belly, and Alice smiled.

"There is that, I suppose. But it could have ended so horribly."

"But it didn't. No use fretting over what will never happen."

Bess was kind to say so, but Alice would never forgive herself.

"What will you do, then?" Bess asked. "Will you truly return home?"

Alice hesitated for a moment. Then she sighed. "I must. I will not let Mary suffer for my sins. My return will surely put a stop to any plans to wed her to Woolsmere. If one of us must be his wife, it will be me. Though I should hope that the scandal of my return will make Woolsmere run far from both of us." She gave Elizabet a faint smile. "Even if it weren't for Mary, I can't stay here forever."

"And why not? John and I would be happy to have you for as long as you'd like. I'll need help when this one comes. I'd like you to be here."

Alice smiled but shook her head. "Being here would mean seeing *him* too often. Glenlyon is too close for comfort. Besides, what use would I be here? I don't know how to do anything. I've never had to do anything for myself, let alone for anyone else."

"Neither had I. You'll learn, as I did."

"Perhaps." She gave Elizabet a wry smile that she hoped hid the sadness that threatened to drown her. "See what I mean about him always being right? I didn't think any of this out. I didn't think of anything besides getting to you. Escaping from a situation I didn't want to be in. I didn't really think how it would affect my parents. Or sweet Mary. I can't prove my suspicions about Lord Woolsmere. Maybe he really is a harmless old man with bad luck in wives. Maybe my fears were nothing more than an ill-prepared girl frightened of her future. Even if he is everything I thought him to be, bringing danger to your door to escape my own was unforgivable."

"Ah, Alice, my dear friend. You are far too hard on yourself."

"Am I? I think I have not been hard enough."

Elizabet hugged her. "Promise me you'll not leave unless you truly wish to. You'll always have a home with me."

"Thank you, Bess. I'll stay. Until this heals, at least," she said, gesturing to her face.

Though she truly meant that she'd stay until she couldn't bear it anymore. She didn't wish to return home, but she wouldn't have many other options if she left Kirkenroch. And despite Elizabet's assurances, she didn't think she'd be able to stay and avoid Philip. Alice had heard the stories. He was John's cousin and close friend. They had ridden together during their highwayman days. Risked their lives for each other countless times. If she were not there, Philip would be living at Kirkenroch, and surely, now that they were all settled, he'd want to help his dearest kinsman rebuild his home. But because of her, he was leaving John's side. He wouldn't be far, true. But Alice's presence was depriving John of a loyal and true brother-in-arms. She didn't have any right to do that.

And she realized that Philip had been right about many things, but one in particular. Her impulsiveness had nearly led to disaster. And she wouldn't be impulsive this time. She'd take the time to carefully weigh her options and decide which was best before she made a decision. Though, since her options were to stay with Elizabet or return home, it really wasn't a difficult decision. But it wasn't one that brought her joy to contemplate.

She could postpone it for a week or two. But she feared the day when she'd have to say goodbye to Kirkenroch forever and return where she belonged.

• • •

The third time Philip dropped his sword, Malcolm shook his head. "No more for today."

Philip wiped his brow, his chest heaving. "I'm fine."

"No, ye're not. Ye havena been fine since ye came back here with yer tail between yer legs, three weeks ago."

Philip glowered at his laird. "Ye ken very well why I returned."

"Aye, I do. Because ye lost yer heart to an English lass and it scares the living piss out of ye."

Philip wasn't sure if he should laugh or challenge Malcolm to a duel for impugning his honor. He finally put down his sword, sighed, and said the only thing he could. "Aye. It does."

Malcolm's eyebrow rose a notch. "I must admit, I didna expect ye to agree so quickly."

Philip shrugged. "It changes nothing."

Malcolm shook his head and wiped the back of his neck with his shirt sleeve. "I need a drink."

He strode back inside, and Philip followed, although if he were wise he'd head for the stables. He'd no wish to hear the lecture Malcolm would soon unleash.

In truth, he'd been repeating the same lecture to himself since the moment he'd ridden away from Kirkenroch. For all the grief he'd given Alice over her impetuous ways, he hadn't spared much thought to leaving her. Oh, he still believed it was the best course of action and had since the moment he'd met her. The problem was, he didn't care anymore. Every time he went outside, his feet invariably took him to the stables. It took more willpower than he could maintain to keep from riding to Kirkenroch and claiming what was his.

He was fairly certain they would drive each other mad within days. But he was also sure that between those moments would be unimaginable pleasure and happiness in each other's arms. Laughter as they butted heads. Excitement, adventure, and utter contentment. They were nothing alike. They looked at the world differently, lived their lives differently. And none of that mattered.

He loved her. He craved her. His life dulled to a meager pretense of an existence without her. And he was done fighting it.

Malcolm downed a tumbler of ale and then turned to Philip. But before The Lion could say a word, Philip laid his sword on the table. "I love her."

Malcolm's eyes widened, and he blinked once or twice before breaking out in a huge grin. "Aye. I've been trying to get ye to see that for weeks."

"I've always seen it. I just didn't want to."

"And that's changed now, has it?"

"Aye."

"Why is that?"

Philip took a deep breath and slowly let it out. "Because I'm a poor, miserable bastard without her."

"Aye, ye are," Malcolm said, clapping him on the back. "What are ye going to do about it?"

Philip gave him a half smile. "I'm going to go and claim my wife. And if that doesna work, I'll beg her to forgive me for being an idiot and pray she's feeling impulsive today."

"What do ye mean, she's gone?" Philip asked, his stomach dropping to his toes as Elizabet looked on with pity-filled eyes.

"I mean, she's gone. She's returned home."

"But…she said she would stay. That she wished to remain here and help you with the babe."

He glanced at the tiny baby James—dubbed wee Jamie by his doting father—who slept peacefully in the cradle beside his mother's chair. He'd been born a few short days after Ramsay's attack and, while he was small, he seemed to be a bonnie, strong lad.

"She said she'd stay for sure only until her bruises healed. But I don't think she'd made any permanent plans after that. To be truthful, I think she was hoping you would come for her. When you didn't…"

John shot his wife a look Philip couldn't read. Not that he put a great deal of effort into it. The sole thought in his head was the realization that he was too late. Alice was gone. He'd waited too long and lost her forever.

"Well," Elizabet continued. "I think she'd hoped to stay longer, but circumstances dictated otherwise."

"When did she leave?" he asked, his voice raw and gruff.

"Yesterday. She received a letter from her sister that informed her that, due to all the fuss and gossip, her parents and Woolsmere did not wish to prolong the engagement. They were receiving a special license, though that is proving somewhat difficult, as she will be Woolsmere's fourth wife. Alice is determined to make sure no harm comes to Mary. In fact, I believe her ship sails from Inverness with the morning tide."

His heart jumped at that. "Her ship doesn't leave until tomorrow? From Inverness?"

Elizabet smiled and nodded. "As you know, Alice isn't the best traveler. We thought it best if she left a day or so ahead of schedule so she'd have plenty of time to make the journey. A fast, more experienced rider would probably make it to the docks before the ship departed. If he left right now…"

Philip grabbed Elizabet and hauled her to him for a quick hug and then sprinted out the door.

John glanced at his wife, his eyebrow cocked. "You forgot to tell him she was most likely coming back once she was assured that Mary was safe from Woolsmere."

"Did I? How forgetful of me."

John chuckled and gave his wife the kiss she deserved.

Chapter Seventeen

Alice stood at the railing of the ship, watching the dock workers scurry to and fro while they finished preparing the ship to sail. The cargo had already been loaded and the gangplank drawn in when a lone rider thundered across the docks. He jumped off the horse and ran to the edge of the dock.

"Alice!"

"Philip?" She gripped the railing and leaned over as far as she dared, her heart nearly hammering out of her chest. "What are you doing here?" she asked.

"Ye said ye werena leaving!"

She shook her head. He came all the way after her to yell at her for leaving? "I have to go to Mary."

He threw up his hands and said something else, but his words were lost in the shouts of the sailors and the grinding and creaking of the ship as the anchor was cranked out of the water on its giant chain.

He waved his arms, shouting up at her, then pacing back and forth on the dock before stopping to shout some more. It looked as if he was trying to stop them from leaving.

Stop *her* from leaving.

The sweet warmth of hope raced through her, melting away the heartbroken ice that had lodged itself in her chest. She grabbed one of the sailors who scurried by.

"Tell the captain he can't leave yet."

The sailor looked at her as if she'd gone mad. "I canna do that, mistress. We've already left."

He pointed to the dock which was now several feet from the ship. She gasped in dismay and gripped the railing again, walking along it as the boat drew farther from shore so she could keep Philip in sight.

Philip paced back and forth a few more times and then finally backed up a few feet, only to go charging back across the dock. Alice screamed as he dove off the dock. Several sailors ran to assist her, but she pushed them all out of the way as she searched the water for Philip.

He bobbed back up near the rear of the ship, and Alice grasped the lapels of the sailor next to her. "Throw down a rope!"

The man seemed so startled he didn't even hesitate to follow her orders. Within a few minutes, they lowered a rope ladder. Philip had fallen farther behind but renewed his efforts at the sight of the ladder, his strong arms cutting through the water until he reached it.

Alice nearly slumped onto the deck, her head spinning with relief when he hauled himself out of the sea. She hung over the railing as far as she dared so she could yell down to him.

"What did you think you were doing? Are you completely mad?"

"Aye! And freezing too. Find me a blanket!" he shouted back to her as he climbed his way up the ladder.

She grasped his shirt as soon as he was close enough and

pulled at him, though her efforts probably hindered more than helped him. The moment he was safely on deck, she threw her arms around him, not caring that freezing ocean water soaked her gown.

His arms wrapped around her, and for a few seconds, she reveled in the blissful feel of his embrace.

Until ten armed sailors surrounded him, shouting for him to step away from her and explain what the hell he was doing aboard their ship. He moved slowly away from her, his hands held up. She wanted to know the answer to that one, too, but he'd have to live long enough to tell her first.

She stepped between him and their guns.

"Alice!" he shouted, but she waved his protests away.

"Put those guns down before you hurt someone!" she yelled. "He's my...my...he's..." She threw her hands up with an exasperated sigh. "He's here for me. He's not going to hurt me."

It took a few more minutes of shouting and arguing before the captain finally believed that the crazy man who'd invaded his ship meant no harm to anyone and ordered his men to stand down. One of them begrudgingly fetched a blanket for Philip, who wrapped it gratefully about his shoulders.

Alice watched all this with impatience, and the moment they were alone on their little corner of the deck, she rounded on him.

"You could have drowned! I don't know what you think you were doing, but I've never seen anyone do something so reckless and dangerous and irresponsible and—"

He laughed. "I think it's a fair sight better than blackmailing a stranger into taking me across the border, so I can go live with an exiled highwayman and his lady."

Her mouth snapped shut. She couldn't argue with that. "I still think you're mad."

"Aye, I am," he said. "But I'm no' completely crazy. I

grew up swimming in the loch by Glenlyon. Fell in once as a lad and my father made certain were it to happen again, I'd be able to save myself."

"Oh," she said, some of the fight going out of her. But once her blood no longer raced with abject terror at his imminent and watery demise, she arched her brows and stepped back.

"Philip. What are you doing here?"

He dropped the blanket and came toward her until he was a few inches from her. Then he took her hands in his.

Her heart jumped at his touch, and she warred between the urge to throw her arms around his neck or yank her hands from his grasp.

"Do ye love me?" he asked.

Her breath caught in her throat, and she searched his face for any sign of what he might be thinking. "Are you ill?" she finally asked. "Did your plunge into the ocean do some irreparable damage?"

"I'm of utterly sound mind, mistress. Ye havena answered me."

"That question doesn't deserve an answer."

"I ken that well. But I'm askin' anyway."

She tried to pull her hands from his, and he let go of one, but only so he could brush a thumb across her cheek.

"What are you doing, Philip?"

"I'm trying to get the woman I love to admit she loves me, too."

Her heart tripped fast enough it made her suck in a breath. "What did you say?"

"I love ye, Alice. I have from the first moment ye looked at me with those laughing, bonnie eyes of yers. Ye blackmailed yer way into my life, and now I find I am yer very willing captive. I want ye with me, as my wife. At my home...well, on my land. I'd have to build ye a home, but I'd build ye one as grand as ye wished if it took me all of my days. Or perhaps at

Kirkenroch, or at Glenlyon, or even in London if that's where ye wish to go."

"You're willing to go to London?"

He grimaced but said, "Aye."

"That's a bit impulsive of you, isn't it?"

Amusement shone from her eyes, and his lips twitched. "Aye. But then, when ye ken something is right, there's no reason to waste a lot of time thinking too long on it."

She'd believed that once, too. And she wanted to believe him. Wanted to believe in this new outlook he seemed to have. But…

"You weren't wrong, you know."

His brow furrowed, and he tilted his head in question.

"We are too different. You were right. About that and all of it. So, what's changed?"

He pulled her closer. "What's changed is I dinna care."

"You don't?"

He shrugged. "I care only that ye are with me the rest of my days. The rest we can figure out. Everyone has problems they must work through. It's what makes life interesting."

"Is that so?" she asked with a laugh.

"Aye. So, I'll ask ye again, my lady. Do ye love me?"

She bit her lip, wanting so badly to say yes, but fearing it all the same.

"I'll probably never do as you bid me."

He chuckled. "Aye, I didna think ye would."

"I'll probably keep making impulsive decisions that will land me in trouble."

"Then I'll have to keep ye by my side so whatever trouble finds ye finds me, too."

She gave him a tremulous smile that grew as she looked into his deep blue eyes. "I'll probably love you until the day I die. And perhaps long after that."

The smile he gave her spread a warmth through her soul

that would never fade. He wrapped his arms around her waist and picked her up. She laughed and wrapped her arms around his neck as his lips met hers.

Someone cleared his throat, and Alice managed to untangle herself from Philip enough to look around and notice a small audience had grown while the man she loved had kissed her silly.

"Is everything all right, my lady?" the captain asked.

Alice stood at Philip's side, hands clasped and eyes shining with happiness.

"Everything is wonderful," Alice said.

"Captain, if you and yer crew wouldna mind standing witness for us…"

The captain looked puzzled but nodded.

"I, Philip Michael Alexander MacGregor, proclaim in front of these witnesses that I love the Lady Alice…"

He glanced at her, and she laughed. "Beatrice." Then she leaned into him and whispered, "Isn't this rather impulsive?"

"Aye, 'tis, and it's high time I did something impulsive," he whispered back. Then to the bewildered audience crowding around them, he continued. "I love the Lady Alice Beatrice Chivers and claim her as my wedded wife."

All eyes turned to Alice, but she had eyes only for Philip. "And I, Lady Alice Beatrice Chivers, proclaim in front of these witnesses that I love Mr. Philip Michael Alexander MacGregor and claim him as my wedded husband."

The sailors erupted in cheers and applause.

Alice laughed and stood on her toes so she could kiss her chosen husband.

"Oh!" she said, pushing away from Philip.

"What is it, lass?" he asked with a slight frown.

"We are on a ship headed to London. I'd hoped to return to Kirkenroch, but Mary… I have to make sure she's all right."

"Ye were going to return?" He laughed softly. "Remind

me to thank Elizabet for leaving that bit of information out."

Alice grinned. "She didn't tell you?"

Philip shook his head and pulled her back into his arms. "Well, no matter. As for London, I suppose ye should introduce yer husband to yer family. This time ye can say a proper goodbye. And perhaps invite them to visit, should they wish. And should we find yer sister to be in any danger, we'll whisk her away with us."

"You'd turn kidnapper for me?"

"Aye, lass. I'd do that and worse. Though perhaps we'll just invite ourselves to stay with the happily wedded couple and ensure that yer sister stays happy."

Alice raised an eyebrow. "For how long?"

"As long as she needs us."

Alice cupped her husband's face in her hands, her heart overflowing. She reached up to kiss him again, sinking in to him as his lips met hers.

And this time Alice knew that irregular or not, their marriage was built to last.

Epilogue

Alice shook her head, watching as her husband meticulously repacked every single item the staff at Oxenwald Court, her sister's new country estate, had already packed.

"There was nothing wrong with that trunk," she pointed out.

"There's no harm in making things a wee bit neater," Philip said.

Alice laughed and wandered back to the window. Mary was still walking in the gardens below, her skirts billowing next to the brightly hued flowers and plants. A young gentleman walked beside her.

Philip joined her at the window. "Are ye sure Mary willna need ye? We can stay longer if ye wish."

Alice shook her head and leaned back against him. "My concerns for her ceased the day Woolsmere died. She's a wealthy widow now, free to do as she wishes."

"Aye, but with her husband's kinsman inheriting the title…will there be any issues with her inheritance? After all, they were married less than a week before he died."

"The contracts were signed and the marriage was blessed in church before dozens of witnesses. Her inheritance is secure. And so is she now. Mary still has this estate and a great deal of money. Besides," she said, nodding in the direction of Mary and the new Lord Woolsmere, "he is a very distant kinsman. And a young and handsome one at that. Perhaps Mary will yet bear an heir for the Woolsmere estate."

Philip snorted and Alice laughed. "In the meantime, she is free of her despicable husband, and with her new wealth and status, she can live her life as she sees fit. Which means I can as well."

"And ye wish to return to Scotland, do ye? Now that yer parents have forced me to wed ye good and proper in the kirk in front of a proper reverend."

"Oh, forced was it?"

"Well, they did keep things rather hushed, though I suppose that stands to reason, as we'd already said we were wed."

"True, but having things done proper with all the right contracts signed and registered made them feel much better about everything. Thank you for indulging them. Forced though you were."

"Aye, well, maybe there wasna so much force as all that needed," he said with a wink.

"*Um hmm.*"

"Especially since they generously offered to release yer dowry as was right and proper and *oof—*"

Alice's elbow connected with his midsection, and he broke off in a grunt that turned into a chuckle.

"Dinna fash, wife. Wild boars couldna have kept me from wedding ye, no matter how many times I must do so."

It was such comments that turned her insides to goo and made her want to follow him to the ends of the earth and back. She brought her hand up to cup his face and rose on her toes to press a gentle kiss to his lips. "Who would have thought you'd have turned into such a willing bridegroom?"

"Aye," he said with a satisfied sigh. "Well, ye do liven up my days, I'll give ye that." He hugged her tightly to him.

She cuddled into him, though she turned her head so she could continue to watch her sister. She wanted nothing more than to be Philip's wife and build a home and family with him. But she would miss her family.

"Are ye sure ye wish to return to Scotland?" he asked her again.

"Aye," Alice said, turning in his arms. "My family here is settled. I'd like to go back, be near Elizabet. And I still worry for Rose. There's been no word yet…"

"That doesna mean they havena returned. Only that word hasn't reached us here."

"I know. But what if they haven't returned yet? What if something has happened to them both? I would like to be close in case I'm needed. Rose risked much for me and mine."

"Then return we shall."

She smiled up at him. "Besides, I know it's where your heart truly lies."

"Nay, lass," Philip said, running a gentle finger down her cheek. "My heart lies with ye, wherever ye may be."

Her heart filled near to bursting, and she shook her head, laughing at herself for turning into such a sap. "Then let's go back to Scotland, husband. It's where we belong."

Acknowledgments

My eternal thanks to my wonderful editor, Erin Molta, who I will always consider my personal fairy godmother. You made my dreams come true and then you helped me make them publishable. I am unbelievably blessed to work with such an amazing editor who cares not only for my books but also keeping me sane while I write them. "Thank you" will never seem sufficient, but I'm going to keep saying it. Huge thanks also to my incredible Entangled team: Alethea Spiridon, you are the goddess. Always. And to Riki Cleveland, my publicists, and everyone at Entangled, I am always blown away by how much effort you put into making each book a success. I am so grateful to be able to work with you all! Sarah Ballance, life has thrown us a few loops and these crazy schedules of ours make me miss you like crazy, but you will always be my #creepytwin! Minus the horror movies because I am terrified just listening to you talk about them! Toni Kerr, thank you for your never-ending support! My sweet family, you are my everything. I hope I make you proud. And to my readers, you make it possible for me to do what I love, and I am humbled and grateful for each and every one of you. Thank you!!

About the Author

Romance and nonfiction author Michelle McLean is a jeans and T-shirt kind of girl who is addicted to chocolate and Goldfish crackers and spent most of her formative years with her nose in a book. She has a B.S. in History, a M.A. in English, loves history and romance, and enjoys spending her time combining the two in her novels.

When Michelle's not editing, reading, or chasing her kids around, she can usually be found in a quiet corner working on her next book. She resides in Pennsylvania with her husband and two children, a massively overgrown puppy, two crazy parakeets, and three very spoiled cats. She also writes contemporary romance as Kira Archer.

Get Scandalous with these historical reads...

CAPTIVATING THE EARL
a *Lords and Ladies in Love* novel by Callie Hutton

To escape her traitorous father's reputation, Lady Elizabeth is hiding as a governess...until Lord Hawkins arrives. Hawk discovers Lizzie's secret and despite orders from the Home Office to bring her in, he vows to protect her. The best way to do that is to make Lizzie his wife, though she adamantly refuses. But someone in the Home Office wants Lizzie dead and Hawk must convince her of the danger when even becoming his countess may not save her life.

THE EARL AND THE RELUCTANT LADY
a *Lords of Vice* novel by Robyn DeHart

From the very moment Agnes Watkins walked into his life, Fletcher Banks, Earl of Wakefield, has wanted her. Agnes is not just beautiful, she's clever and determined. Despite her uncommon beauty, she refuses to conform to society's standards. She's also the sister of the man who holds Fletcher's career as a spy in his hands. And that makes her completely off-limits. But the more time they spend together, the harder it is to deny that this infatuation may be more than lust...

A ROGUE FOR EMILY
a *Lady Lancaster Garden Society* novel by Catherine Hemmerling

Alex would rather be doing anything other than escorting the high and mighty Emily, until a secret about her falls into his lap. Suddenly, he realizes there may be more to the lady than he originally thought. Perhaps the only thing that can keep them from killing each other is falling for each other instead.

CPSIA information can be obtained
at www.ICGtesting.com
Printed in the USA
LVHW041520140219
607564LV00001B/39/P

9 781794 406742